JILLEEN DOLBEARE

Splintered Destiny

VINCI
BOOKS

By Jilleen Dolbeare

Vinci Books

vinci-books.com

Published by Vinci Books Ltd in 2025

1

The publisher and the author have made every effort to obtain permissions for any third party material used in this book and to comply with copyright law. Any queries in this respect should be brought to the attention of the publisher and any omissions will be corrected in future editions.

A CIP catalogue record for this book is available from the British Library.

Paperback ISBN: 9781036706128

Chapter One

Gabe was acting strange. He paced, he looked nervous, and he kept trying to talk, but repeatedly stopped after a word or two. I didn't know what was wrong.

"I know both of us had bad marriages," he started.

My heart sank and I felt sick. Was he breaking up with me? Did he choose this vacation as a way to say, "Your life is too crazy, I'm out?"

I was already dressed for dinner, but my ankles weren't going to hold me up in these shoes with the gut punch that was coming. After having one relationship come to a shocking end, I expected the worst. I didn't know if I would survive him leaving me. I sat heavily on the edge of the bed and breathed quickly then held my breath and focused on keeping it together—showing dignity. I gripped the bedspread so tightly my hands ached.

"I wish that I'd been smart enough to track you down earlier." Gabe pulled his shirt collar away from his throat. I could see the stress in his tight movements.

Maybe I was wrong. I let my breath go and took a few

deep, cleansing ones. I released the death grip on the bedspread. Maybe he wasn't breaking up with me. That meant… My heart raced. My palms started to sweat. Was he…?

"I didn't think I'd ever want to try again, but if you're willing, there just isn't anyone else for me."

My breath caught in my throat. My hand moved of its own volition to cover my mouth. My heart began to flutter in my chest. I was either having a heart attack or an extreme case of the butterflies.

His hand shook as he pulled out the small box from his jeans pocket. I was glad I was sitting because I felt weak, and I knew my legs wouldn't hold me. I swallowed, my throat suddenly dry.

He knelt and handed me the open box. "Brigid Donovan, will you marry me?"

He looked straight at me. His heart shined in his hazel eyes, the candlelight gleaming off the moisture filling them.

My hand shook, but I reached down and took the box, my eyes never leaving his. I swallowed the lump that was closing off my throat. We'd been through so much together, and the love I felt for him was big. Bigger than I was. I couldn't even contain it in my body—it spilled out like the uncontrolled tears now running down my face.

I blinked them away and stared at the ring, glittering against the black velvet lining of the box. The ring was perfect. It wasn't a diamond, thank heavens. Gabe knew better. He knew I had weird superstitious feelings about diamonds—especially after my first marriage and the issues with my ice magic. It was hard to get over being beaten, having the magic taken from me, and only getting it back after several murder attempts. The ongoing battles over it with Sofia made me a little weird about diamonds. The ring sparkled in the candlelight. It was a large, round cut sapphire surrounded by white gold and intricate filigree. It was exquisite and perfectly me.

"Yes!" I sobbed.

I threw my arms around his neck while still holding the box. He stood up, pulled me off my feet, and kissed me soundly. He twirled us around, my hair flowing around my head like the dress's skirt floated around my knees as we both laughed and cried together. Once he put me down, he plucked the ring out of the box and placed it on my finger. I admired it for a moment and then kissed him again. The smile hurt my cheeks as the tears fell.

"I wish I'd done this when we were eighteen; it would have saved us both a bunch of heartache," he said.

"We couldn't have known, but I agree."

He nodded and looked down at his watch, "Are you ready to go?"

I wiped my cheeks. "Just give me a moment." I hurried to the bathroom and cleaned up my smeared mascara. I felt like skipping and would have if my feet ever touched the ground again. I walked out, smiled, and held up my ring-bedecked hand. "All fancied up and ready to roll!"

He grinned, the tension disappearing from his shoulders, and grasped my hand to stare at the ring. Then he pulled me in for another hug and kiss.

We were on vacation, just the two of us. After all that had happened, we needed time away. At least, I needed it. After the last vampire attack, I'd closed the inn. It was too dangerous for my patrons, and the house had been damaged. Gabe found us a lovely resort to escape to in Riviera Maya, Mexico.

Mr. Mittens was holding down the fort back home, although he'd protested mightily about us going where he couldn't protect me. I told him I was a realm walk away and could be home at the first sign of any trouble. That *hadn't* mollified him. I had to promise to call Megan every day and check in. He'd have demanded I call him directly if he had pockets for a phone.

It was hard to leave him behind, but I needed to get away. I needed time with Gabe, and I needed to remember what it was like to be human—even if I wasn't. I had to let the stress go, or my magic wouldn't be the only thing acting wacky in my life. Since Dana had unblocked my magic, it was unstable but *stronger*.

Gabe took me to a fancy restaurant. It was in the resort, so it wasn't authentic Mexican food, but good food was good food. We'd been here two days.

I was excited about the proposal and unbelievably happy. My face ached from smiling, and having alone time with Gabe was everything. Still, in the back of my mind, I had to keep telling myself to relax, enjoy, and soak in the love.

I *tried* to be normal. I really did. I'd put on my game face and acted happy as hard as I could. We ate, we swam, we danced, we made love. I should be enjoying Gabe, the proposal, our time alone, but I still couldn't relax.

I didn't think I ever would until the vampires were gone and the griffins had been dealt with.

Gabe gave it a good try—ignoring my agitation—until he finally said, "Look, I know you can't stop thinking about everything. Let's just go home."

I felt terrible. He'd planned such a wonderful time and loved me so much. I loved him and wanted him to be happy as well.

His decision only added to my stress. I was mucking up everything—my life, my business, my relationship. Even my cat was affected. The worst thing? I had *no* answers. I couldn't fix *anything*; I had no idea how to stop the vampires or mollify the griffins. But what really bothered me was I needed to take care of it fast before it came back to bite us all. Until then, I felt guilty having the time of my life. We packed up our stuff, and rather than take the plane home—my dumb idea to feel normal on the way here—I realm walked us back.

Mr. Mittens was happy, but I wasn't sure about anyone else. They were all in a holding pattern, waiting for me to either reopen the B&B or fire them all. That was another layer of stress. I wanted the B&B to flourish. I planned to reopen, and firing my staff wouldn't help in the long run. I'd have to start over—again. Plus, they relied on me for a job, for pay, and in the case of Jim and Chef Jack, for housing as well. When I thought of it, I started to hyper-ventilate.

Since the last attack two weeks earlier, no one had seen or heard from a single vampire or griffin. My staff kept looking at me sideways, trying to guess my next steps. In truth, if I were fully human, I'd probably need blood pressure medication. I might be independently wealthy, but at some point, I'd need an income to support it all. The B&B was my answer. I just needed it to be a functional business again.

Sorcha, my baincapall friend from Faerie, had added four more to her patrol. At least they didn't care if I reopened or not. It was easier protecting fewer people. Mr. Mittens didn't care about the inn, although he cared about its people, mainly me—and Megan, by default. He hadn't said much about Gabe, but I think he was keeping an eye on him, trying to determine if he was safe and good for me. That's the sense I got, anyway.

Once I gathered Megan and Mr. Mittens together, I sprang the news on them. "We're engaged!"

Hmpf, was Mr. Mittens' response, and then satisfied I was home, he wandered away to do his own stuff. I expected more from him. He was acting weird. Maybe there was jealousy?

Megan's response was more normal. She shrieked so loud, I jumped, and ran at me, holding out her hands in the "gimme" position. "Congratulations! That's magnificent! Let me see the ring." Then she dove for my hand aggressively.

I held it out, beaming, for her inspection.

"Wowzer, that's some rock! I love the sapphire, it's *so* you."

"I know. It's perfect; Gabe is perfect."

"Tell me everything, leave no detail out."

"Uh, everything?"

She rocked her hand back and forth. "If you must edit…I guess I'll live."

I laughed and told her about how nervous he had been and that I thought he was like that because he was trying to break up.

"No way."

"Yes, way."

"That boy adores you. He wouldn't break up!" she insisted.

"Well, my life is crazy. He's been kidnapped twice because of me and had to fight vampires. I wouldn't blame *anyone* for running as far away from me as possible."

"That's Evan messing with your mind."

"What? No. I don't think about Evan," I said.

"Because he messed you up. So, stop. Gabe isn't Evan, and he wouldn't leave you."

I looked her in the eye. She was deadly serious. Her surety helped settle my tension a micro amount. She could be right. I didn't have great judgment, or at least judgment I trusted, and I knew that was a result of the emotional abuse. There was also that pesky fact that Evan had dumped me for his pregnant girlfriend, which didn't help my trust issues.

"You are probably right. I am a bit of a mess. Thanks, I couldn't pinpoint why I've been so…" I shrugged. I couldn't think of the words.

"Stupid?" Megan supplied, smiling.

I laughed. "Yeah, perfect answer."

"So, is he moving in?"

"Yeah, he has the time off now since we were supposed to be gone longer. He went home to start packing. I'm going to put my stuff away and clear some space for him."

"Want help?"

"Sure!"

She followed me into my bedroom, which was soon to be mine and Gabe's. I looked around. A momentary sense of trepidation overwhelmed me. Megan caught my expression.

"What's wrong?" she asked, alarmed.

"It's nothing." I shook my head and waved the question away.

"I know you; you can't get away with that."

"It's just a stupid selfish feeling. It'll pass."

"What is it?"

I sighed and felt a flush of embarrassment. "I just had a moment where I didn't want anything to change. This is my first space all on my own, and other than Mr. Mittens, I haven't had to share it for almost a year now."

She was quiet for a moment. "That's normal. At least, it's hard to combine your life with someone else's no matter

7

how much you care for or love them. I know. You'll get over it once you adjust."

I smiled at her gratefully. "Yeah, I know. It *is* just an adjustment, and I'm happy. I told you it was dumb."

"Feelings aren't dumb. They just are. You're doing the right thing with the right person. It'll be great."

"OK, no more maudlin moments. Let's work!"

We started moving things around and making space. Of course, that's when the griffins decided to come back.

Chapter Two

Mr. Mittens droll voice in my head was what alerted me. *Brigid, you have winged visitors.*

"Not bats?" I asked, worried it was vampires.

No, griffins. I'll warn Brightfeather.

"Thanks."

I looked up at Megan—I didn't know if that was a wide broadcast by my cat or just to me. She hadn't flinched, so I said, "We have incoming griffins."

She sighed. "I was enjoying the break from the crazy."

"Me too."

We hurried out the back. Sure enough, a contingent of griffins was landing in the parking lot. At least there weren't guest vehicles to get in the way. Their royal pains in the ass were with the usual entourage of courtiers. I didn't know what the griffins called them, but my time in the high court of Faerie had added a whole litany of new words to my vocabulary.

Thorn and his mate Firial, the king and queen, stepped forward once they saw me.

"Your Majesties," I said. "Welcome back. I'd like to thank you formally for your assistance with the vampires."

They gave me stiff nods in acknowledgement. However, I sincerely doubted they were here only to receive my thanks. This had to do with Brightfeather. I think they were suspicious. I didn't know if they guessed about the chicks, but they had to know something was going on, or they wouldn't keep coming back.

"I've summoned Brightfeather, if that is the purpose for your visit?"

It is. Our son's mate should attend us at our court. We will request her presence.

I was afraid of this. Brightfeather couldn't leave her chicks. If she didn't go, she'd be offending the royals, and they could demand her presence. A conundrum. I didn't see a way she could get around this without telling them about her babies.

I felt a pulse of magic, and Mr. Mittens appeared next to me on his usual perch on the railing of the back porch.

Brightfeather is flying in. The chicks are asleep, Mr. Mittens said.

"It's not good, Mr. Mittens," I said silently.

His head lowered. He liked Brightfeather, and he was an honorary uncle to the griffin chicks. He knew the stakes. We all did. He'd fight as hard as the rest of us if we had to.

I could hear the distant beats of griffin wings, and soon enough, a shadow brushed past us as Brightfeather back-winged into the narrow space left by the crowd of griffins.

She landed and bowed before the royals. *How may I serve you?*

The griffin royals gave no preamble. The queen stated, *As the mate of our only son, we require you to return and take up his royal duties.*

My heart sank, and a frisson of fear blasted through me. We hadn't thought of this possibility.

Brightfeather looked stunned. I didn't think she'd thought of this possibility either. She knew they'd want to take the babies, but not her. Either scenario was a disaster. She threw a glance my way. Pure panic burned in her eyes.

"If I may, Your Majesties, Brightfeather has been my main general in the fight against the vampires. Could I beg for her continued assistance for a short time?"

They looked at each other, Brightfeather's eager gaze on them. She still looked rough. Losing her mate, and then taking care of three growing and rambunctious chicks was taking a toll.

They must have been communicating silently to each other, because Thorn spoke. *We will give you one month. Then, you must return.*

Brighfeather bowed her head in submission. I could sense her growing panic. *I will comply,* she said. She had no choice. From what she'd told me, their word was law, and they enforced it with deadly effectiveness.

They nodded to her, and the whole group lifted off the ground in a single leap, the whoosh of their wings nearly flattening us. We watched from the porch until the griffins were nothing but dots in the sky.

What am I going to do? Brightfeather cried.

"We have a month. We'll come up with something. Until then, take care of those babies. We aren't going to let the king and queen take your babies from you." I looked her in the eye so she could see I meant it. My friends had become closer than family. I didn't want to lose any of them.

She took a deep shaky breath. *Thanks, Brigid. That helps.*

11

You're right. We have some breathing room to figure this out. She leapt high into the air and flew off towards her nest.

I looked at my cat. "Have you taken meat to them lately? She looks awful."

I have. I hunt for them every other day. His tone was disdainful, like how *dare* I ask.

"I wasn't trying to insult you; I was just worried about Brightfeather," I said, trying to soothe his hurt feelings. He must have forgiven me, because he gave me a head butt. "Come inside, I want to talk to you about something."

He jumped down and strolled into the kitchen with me. He sprang up on the old kitchen table. It had been in this house since it was built, and all my family that had lived in this house had used it. It was a huge, solid farm table, and I loved it.

Mr. Mittens gazed at me, patiently waiting to see what I was going to tell him.

"Gabe is moving in," I blurted out. I didn't know why it was hard to tell him, other than I wasn't sure if he approved.

He blinked once, slowly. *That is all?*

He hadn't reacted like I thought. My cat was keeping secrets. I sensed he knew before I did that Gabe was going to propose. I narrowed my eyes at him. "Yeah, why?"

He looked away and licked a patch of hair as though it was bothering him more than usual. It was one of his tells, he was nervous. He also sounded more smug than usual. *You acted like it was something earth shattering. I was expecting a new invasion by yet a third race of dangerous creatures from this planet.*

"I thought it was big news." My tone was a little snippy. Something was going on; I'd get to the bottom of it.

Congratulations. He jumped down and strolled into the

front, escaping before I could question him about his shifty behavior.

I followed, because I still wasn't finished with my project, and I didn't know when Gabe would show.

Does this require me to move my bed? he asked.

I cringed. I hadn't even thought about it. But with two adult people, his large cat bed smack in the middle of the bed would have to be moved. When Gabe stayed on other occasions, Mr. Mittens just disappeared. That would be harder now that Gabe was going to be here fulltime.

"Probably, but it doesn't have to go far, just to a different spot."

He gave me a cat nod and wandered off. I think I'd hurt his feelings. I looked on my phone to see what the largest bed I could order was. My current mattress was king size, and Mr. Mittens and I were fine. Gabe would be crowded if the cat bed remained. There was a bed called an Alaskan king. It was almost two feet longer and wider than the regular king. Nine feet square. It was a good thing I had an extremely large room. The sheets must be like tents. It could be delivered in a few days, so I ordered it with a smile. I wanted to surprise my cat.

Gabe already knew that Mr. Mittens and I were a package deal. Plus, he was grateful to the cat for protecting me. I smiled at this, then frowned as I thought about what was before us.

Mr. Mittens and I had decided to take the fight to the vampires, but even though it had been two weeks since that decision, we still didn't have a plan. The link to Faerie gave this land free energy which kept us powered up. We both needed it. But we had no way to take it with us.

I'd given the problem to Dana, my great-grandfather's mistress of magic, but even though she was a master at making portable magic, she hadn't come up with a solution either. I thought, naively, that she'd be able to make a portable magic ball we could tap into, but apparently it didn't work that way.

Vamps grew stronger as they aged. They lost their sensitivity to sunlight and could shapeshift into more dangerous forms. Most young vamps could turn into bats, but they were small and almost harmless alone. Although when they swarmed, it was terrifying. The ancient ones could turn into man-sized vampire bats—absolutely horrific creatures with boundless strength and very bad attitudes. We believed Vic had exhausted his supply of ancient vamps when he threw them at us the last time, and we'd removed Bella from that lineup.

I sighed, exhausted from thinking about it and worrying about it for so long. I needed that vacation I'd cut short. I'm sure Gabe did, too. I sat on my bed. I would just lay down for a second...

Chapter Three

I woke up with Gabe shaking me gently.

"Sorry, Bridge, but Megan has something important to tell us."

I struggled up. Gabe gave me a hand. I couldn't believe how tired I was. Too much worry, too much stress.

"What's up?"

"I'm not sure, something to do with Goch, and well, let's go out and let her explain. I'm not sure I understand what she was saying."

I stretched and followed him out. She was standing on the back porch. Goch was in the parking lot—no squished vehicles. He'd finally learned to avoid them, I hoped.

"What's up?" I asked. "Gabe said you had something to tell us."

Megan danced around, her eyes twinkling like she was going to burst out of her skin. "This is exactly what we need; you have to hear this story!"

I was too tired for this. I looked between her and Goch.

The teenage dragon looked pleased with himself, so I gave him my attention. I sat down on the porch steps.

"Ok, Goch, tell Brigid what you told me," Megan commanded.

The dragon's eyes glowed golden with pleasure. He loved being helpful. *Megan said that you were looking for a way to keep your power filled away from this land.*

"Yes, for me and Mr. Mittens," I answered, confused.

Well, the dragons have a legend. His tail whipped back and forth, and I grew concerned he would break something. *Long ago, there was a golden collar that had a huge red stone on it. It was said it could harness energy and be manipulated by the dragon wearing the collar. That's the way we'll be able to beat the vampires! We'll get the collar, and then you'll have access to your power wherever we go!*

I shook my head. My dragon charge was enthusiastic and willing to do almost anything for us, even letting us ride him when we needed a lift to Faerie, but this sounded too much like the other type of fairy tale.

"Goch, do you know if the collar really exists? It could just be a myth or legend." I wanted to let him down easily.

It's not a myth. I've seen it! I know where it is!

I looked at Gabe. He seemed as mystified as me.

"Just listen," Megan said. "Let him finish, you'll understand!"

"Where? When?" I asked Goch.

When I was a hatchling. My mother took me to the elders. She wanted their blessings for me. She talked to them while I waited. I wandered off and got lost in the caves. I wandered for a long time, and in one of the deep spaces, I saw it. A great golden collar with a large red gem. It was in the elder's hoard.

"Their hoard? Won't they be loath to part with it?" I asked.

I don't know. If it will help me and my friends and we bring it back, why would they mind?

I sighed. The sweet dragon was a bit naïve. But it was interesting. And an option we hadn't had before.

"Megan, is there any guarantee this collar will do what we want it to do?" I asked quietly so Goch wouldn't hear. He seemed so happy to have an idea.

"Nope. But it exists. That's a chance, and it's not like we have any other ideas."

She had me there. I looked at Gabe. "What do you think?"

He shrugged. "I think if we want to take the fight to the vamps, and not be sitting here waiting for them to destroy us, we should check it out."

I nodded. It seemed I was outvoted. Plus, there was the tiny spark of hope flaring to life in my belly. Maybe this was the answer.

"Ok, Goch. Tell us all you know."

His tail swished again, and his eyes lit up. *The stories say the gem can hold as much magic as you can fill it with. Dragon mages have a lot of power. It has to be able to help you and Mr. Mittens! There's a story that my mother told me when I was young. About how the collar was used to save the dragons long ago. There was this human mage, I think his name was Merson...*

"Merlin?" Megan interrupted.

Yes, that's right! Do you know him?

We looked at each other and laughed. "We've heard stories about him. He's probably the most famous earth mage."

Oh! He seemed deflated. Then perked back up. *He helped make the collar for the dragons! I think he called it an amerset? I don't know the word in English.*

"Amulet?"

Yes, that's it!

I was growing more and more excited. An amulet created by Merlin? Could it be the real deal?

"And you're sure we can borrow it?"

He paused. *No, I'm not sure, but it's important. So, they have to let us, right?*

"I don't think so, Goch, but we'll ask."

I'm a dragon, so I don't think it will be a big deal.

I laughed at his use of "big deal." He'd been hanging with us for so long, he'd picked up everyday usage in the language. It was cute.

However, I believed it would be a "big deal" to the dragons. An amulet created by Merlin? It sounded like a highly guarded treasure. Still, what choice did we have if we were to defeat the vampires?

I looked at Gabe, Megan, and Goch. I guess this motley crew was going on a quest.

Chapter Four

I don't understand, Mr. Mittens said. *Who?*

"Merlin. He was the greatest enchanter who ever lived."

A magic user like you?

I thought about that for a minute. I had no idea if Merlin was actually human. In the legends, he had some links to Faerie beings. Maybe he had been Fae himself? I didn't know.

"I don't really know. I guess he could have been Fae."

If he was, this could be good. It might already be something you can use, he said sagely. *And if it's Fae magic, I can also access it. Of course, I could access human magic if it was strong enough*, he added thoughtfully. *Is there a human magic source? Could you access it if we could find one?*

My cat often thought up more interesting questions than I did. I'd never considered that a human magic source might exist. There were human magic users like the witches, but their magic came from an internal well not an outside source. However, that didn't mean that other magic users were the same. I'd never met another one that wasn't a witch. Even the Whelans' Aunt Zella had Fae blood powering her ability to handle ghosts.

It seemed, long ago, Fae had wandered the earth begetting children everywhere. But earth's magical field was weak, according to Mr. Mittens. We just didn't know if we could find a big enough source of earth magic to support my magic and Mr. Mittens', who also came from a magically saturated world.

Maybe the gargoyles knew something. They had said once that they were "created," which meant someone on earth had some power. I stood up suddenly.

Gabe reached out and grabbed my hand. "I know that look. You just had an idea."

I smiled at him. "I did." I looked at Megan. "This is going to need your dragon riding skills."

"I knew you'd see the light!" she said, excitedly. "Goch and I are the best rider and dragon ever!"

"On Earth or Pern?" I asked facetiously.

"Both, duh."

"Yeah, but you don't fight thread here."

"No, and Goch doesn't have to chew firestone. Because he's an Earth dragon, not a genetically modified Pern firelizard."

"True." I smiled at her. She was living her dreams.

"So, what do I, the great dragonrider, need to do?"

"The first part of the quest."

"Quest? Whoa, we're taking this to the next level."

"It was your dragon's idea in the first place, I'm just adding on."

She rubbed her hands together, her eyes glinting. The glee coming off of her was almost tangible. "So, what is our quest?"

"Well, I need to check with the gargoyles first, but it might be to seek the source of magic that created them."

"Shit, that is a good quest. I wonder if I need to order armor."

"You don't already have some?" I mocked her.

"Well…"

I rolled my eyes. "Dana made you a set and put it in a magic ball, didn't she?"

"Not exactly, it's more of a personal ward."

"She's already crafting wards at that level?"

"You know her, she's a bit of an overachiever." Megan shrugged.

"I'd say."

"So, are you calling Sam?"

I smiled and held up the phone, then I pulled up my contacts and chose Sam's number. The gargoyles were due to visit next week. I'd promised them a retreat here for helping us with the vampires, and since the inn was officially closed, I had the space to host them. Every room would be filled and the stables, too. Apparently, some of the gargoyles were permanently locked in their gargoyle form. I didn't have the story about why, but Sam had asked if they could stay as well. It worked best to put them up in the stables. Their stone forms were too heavy for regular beds.

"This is Sam."

"Hi, Sam, it's Brigid. I was hoping to ask you a few questions if you have time?"

"Hey, Brigid. I'd love to help you, but I'm a little busy right now. Can it wait until next week?"

I thought hard. The faster we did everything, the sooner our lives could go back to normal, and the less likely we were to be overrun by vampires. But I couldn't make him answer questions if he didn't have time. He was a friend and ally.

"Sure, no problem. See you next week!"

"Sorry, Brigid, just super busy, also trying to plan our getaway at the inn."

"I get it! No worries."

He hung up. Damn. "Megan, your separate quest is delayed."

"I heard. Oh well, we'll work on the one to get the amulet."

I nodded and smiled at her. She was the best friend ever. Always willing, always fun, always there when I needed her. She'd changed her whole life and belief structure for me. She'd entered a world of magic without a second thought or a look back. My heart swelled with love.

Gabe pulled me against his side, and my heart swelled further. What would I do without the people in my life? I included Mr. Mittens, Goch, and Brightfeather in that as well. I'd also grown to realize that true friends didn't only have two legs either.

Chapter Five

We needed supplies for caving. Goch had been a lot smaller when he'd found the amulet, however, it seemed reasonable to assume the caverns would be large enough for a dragon since they didn't have teleportation skills. Although, Goch could realm walk. Hmmm. Maybe all dragons could? Something to think about.

We couldn't realm walk directly to the amulet. We didn't have a clear enough picture to do so. Also, it wouldn't be prudent to make enemies with the dragons. This called for diplomacy. We needed to beg for their help. Goch wasn't much help in preparation. He was a kid in dragon years and didn't know much beyond rudimentary ideas of their political structure.

The other dragon we knew was his mother, but only because she'd shown up and begged him to return. I was afraid if we went to her, she'd demand he stay with the dragons in exchange for her help. Then again, we had no one else.

Gabe, Megan, and I gathered in the kitchen. Mr. Mittens wandered in just in time for the discussion.

"We can appeal to Goch's mother," I said, thoughtfully.

"Do you think that's a good idea?" Megan asked.

I shrugged.

"She's the only other dragon we know," Gabe added, which was true, and had been my point.

"I guess we need to go to her, but I don't know how to contact her. Hopefully, Goch does."

She's a dragon queen, Mr. Mittens said.

"What?" I asked.

She's a gold. Golden dragons are always queens.

"For real? Just like Pern?" Megan asked, breathless in her excitement.

I do not know that realm, but here, on this planet, gold dragons are queens. Her name practically screams it at you, he added.

I thought for a moment. "Aurora Golden Scales. I don't get 'queen' from that."

Aurora is the name of a goddess in your mythology. Also, it is the crown in the night sky. Queen, he said matter-of-factly.

"Well, damn. I didn't put that together."

Also, Goch told me. Part of why he is rebelling. He does not wish to be part of the royal structure. As a red, he would be a consort to a queen. It is expected of him to mate with one, Mr. Mittens added.

"How many queens are there?" Megan asked. I guess in all her plotting with Goch, she hadn't asked about his background.

I do not know, but I think they are rare. His mother may be the queen, not just a queen.

"I wonder if this will make it harder to see her?" Megan paced back and forth.

Goch is her son. However, she is the one we'll need to appeal to for access to the hoard, Mr. Mittens added.

24

That made sense to me. "Ok, sounds like a plan."

We all agreed. We'd get our supplies, be ready, and ask for her help. So, I sat down with Gabe and Megan, and we started searching the internet.

"I think we need those helmet things with the lights." Megan mimed putting a helmet on her head.

"We'll need rope and rappelling equipment," Gabe added.

"Have you rappelled before?" I asked him.

"I've been a couple of times, but I'm not good enough to be in charge of it. We either need to hire someone, or take some lessons before we go," he added.

"We don't even know if we'll have to rappel." Megan went over to the sink and got a glass of water.

"True. We should scope out the area before we do that. So, lights, helmets, and go from there?" I confirmed.

They agreed.

"When do we want to do this? The gargoyles have their reunion here next week. We have thirty days to find an answer for Brightfeather, and we don't know when the vampires will come after us again. I think we need to visit the dragons soon." I gestured for her to bring me a glass of water as well.

"Yeah, we do. Like tomorrow." She filled a glass and handed it to me.

"Definitely go talk to Goch's mom tomorrow," Gabe added.

I sipped my water. "Who wants to go?"

"I'll have to go another time; I'm back on shift tomorrow," Gabe said.

"I'm free, plus I'm the only dragon rider."

I rolled my eyes. "You are not a dragon rider," I said for the umpteenth time.

She grinned. "I am too. I have a dragon; we fly together."

I sighed. "Whatever. I guess we do have to ride the dragon. We don't know where to go otherwise."

"That's what I'm saying."

"Ugh." I looked at my cat. "Are you coming?"

He cocked his head. *I cannot help. I'll be unable to transform off this land.*

"You could transform before we go."

He froze.

I'd been thinking about this for a while. His only magical power was shapeshifting. I didn't know if his healing was magical or just part of his natural makeup.

I will stay here. We still have vampires and griffins dropping by, he said. *Besides, Megan's harness is not fitted for a cat.*

"True." He did have me there, but I was starting to wonder if something else was bothering my cat. I decided to ponder on it and ask him later.

You should take a gift, he added.

"Gift? What do you take a dragon?" What would a huge scaly winged creature desire?

How would I know? I'm a cat. You humans do gifts, he said and strolled off, his tail straight up, swaying with his movement.

Chapter Six

The next day, Megan put the harness on Goch. I decided not to order anything—not even caving helmets with lights —until we'd seen the dragon caves. We didn't really know what we'd need, and nothing would get here in time, anyway. We had my light magic, and Megan could take a flashlight. It was time to face the queen of the dragons.

As Megan directed Goch where to place his feet and when to stretch his neck, I questioned him about his mother.

"Why didn't you tell us you were a prince?" I asked.

Males aren't royalty unless they mate a queen, he answered.

"So, you aren't considered a prince?"

No, we don't have princes. He lifted his front right foot, and Megan slipped the harness over it.

"But your mom is a queen?"

She is our queen. He put his other foot into the harness.

"Will she be upset that we are riding you?" I was worried it might be considered demeaning in their culture.

I do not think so? he said, although I heard the question in his voice. *Long ago, there were dragons that had riders. Your famous enchanter was one.*

"Merlin was a dragonrider like me? That's so cool!" Megan pumped her first in excitement.

"Great, now I'll never hear the end of it," I mumbled, but I was secretly happy for her. This really was Megan's dream come true.

She snapped the last of the fastenings together and checked that they were secure.

"Well, it's ready. I guess we'll find out soon whether she'll approve or not."

Even though it was a warm summer day, we put on our warmest jackets. It was cold up high, and apparently, the dragon home caves were chilly. I checked that I had the gift Mr. Mittens insisted I take to the dragons. I patted it—it was nestled securely in my pocket—and we climbed onto Goch's broad back.

We assumed take-off position, lying across Goch's back. This was the position we decided on to reduce whiplash. It seemed to work. His powerful muscles bunched, and then he launched himself in the air, beating his mighty wings. Once his flight stabilized, we sat up. Megan seemed comfortable in the air. Of course, she'd been practicing with Goch and was actually quite a natural at dragon riding. I clung to the harness like a tick. I wasn't going to go anywhere whether I held on or not, but it felt more secure. I struggled to look down; the heights were dizzying and terrifying, but I made myself. The view of my land was spectacular, mostly woods, but you could see the massive roof of the house, and after a few wingbeats, the neat fields and buildings of the old dairy.

Goch's mental voice filled my mind, and probably Megan's. *Are you ready to realm walk?*

Megan gave him three thuds on his back, and I felt the warm magic pulse. We flew over the Fae practice planet. The next second, the air was cool and moist, and we soared above our own realm, although far from home. Below us was a rocky and forested island with large mountains. It was overcast, but not solidly, and slips of sunlight moved as we winged closer to the island. I looked as best as I could with the naked eye, but I didn't see any obvious human habitations. We soared through a cloud, the wet air slapped against us, and it took my breath. My hair felt damp, and the stray pieces that had escaped my braid stuck to my face.

When we broke through, I could see the coast more clearly. It appeared there was a logging operation, but the island was mostly empty of anything remotely human. Besides the forest, it was dominated by soaring cliffs. As we approached, I could see the massive caves. Dragon caves.

My heart sped up in anticipation. Goch trumpeted. I could feel his muscles contract with the effort, and the sound was deafening. An answering bugle came from the island. We dove. My stomach stayed in the clouds, and I was amazed when my heart stayed in my chest. We stopped several hundred feet above the mountains and did whatever the closest thing to hovering was for a dragon. Three dragons came up from below, their jeweled tones catching stray sunbeams through the thick clouds—sapphire, emerald, amethyst. They rose up to join us.

The dragons conversed out loud, but since we didn't speak dragon, we had no idea what was being said. However, the new dragons kept looking at us angrily. One spat a brief stream of fire, but it wasn't aimed at us, luckily. Another peeled off the group. The emerald dragon dove to the caves, and it was clear the other two were there to hold us until the emerald had reported in.

They are being dicks, Goch said into our minds with a huff.

I wanted to laugh. He had picked that phrase up from Megan for sure.

"Who are they?" I asked.

My mother's guards. They are upset because I left the wing, and they are treating me like an outsider. They were also not very nice about you riding me, he added. *They called me something very mean in dragon.* He sounded sulky and confused.

This probably wasn't a good idea, I thought just as two more dragons came rocketing out of the caves towards us.

The sun caught them, and it was clear that the emerald was bringing the queen. Her golden scales caught the stray sunbeams and sent blinding rainbows shooting off in all directions. From this angle, it was clear why she was the queen. Not only was she beautiful, she was larger than any of the other dragons. The green dragon struggled to keep up with her sweeping wing beats, and I could feel Goch tremble beneath me.

Was she angry? I gulped and held on tighter to the harness. I wished Megan and I could communicate telepathically, but I hadn't added that ability to her charm. I'd have to fix that; it would make things easier when flying since the wind whipped our words away.

Goch had been lazily soaring on a thermal, using barely a wing beat as he let the air hold us while we circled our patch of sky. The other two dragons did the same below us. As Aurora Golden Scales rose, Goch beat his wings, and the other two joined him so we formed a triangle in the sky. She rose to our level, still in vertical form, while we were flat, and trumpeted before she zipped past us higher and higher until she was a speck. She did a graceful maneuver in the air, added a pirouette, then faced downward and plummeted back to our height, leveling out her flight. It was a spectacular display of aerial mastery.

My son! she said joyfully into our minds.

The tightness in my gut and shoulders eased. Thank heavens, she was happy he'd come to see her.

They chatted in dragon, and we plunged down towards the caves. I guess we'd secured an invite.

Chapter Seven

The entry looked way too small, but Aurora Golden Scales soared through easily, her wingtips almost brushing the edges. I closed my eyes as Goch followed. Inside was the most enormous cavern I could have ever imagined. Several dragons could fly inside at once. Several were perched on stalagmites, resting or grooming, their jeweled tones duller in the darkness of the cave. We flew past them through a tunnel barely large enough for the massive wingspan of the queen, and then we flew into another chamber. The other three dragons stayed behind, and we found ourselves alone with the queen.

She settled on a stone dais—a natural throne. Goch landed, and we unclipped and slid down his offered front leg. My anxiety returned; facing the queen like this was intimidating. My legs were shaky and tight like I'd ridden a horse all day. Goch folded his wings tight once we were off and sat much like Mr. Mittens did, with his tail wrapped around his front feet.

The huge golden dragon gazed down on us. *My son says you've come to ask a boon of the dragons.*

I took a step forward and gave her my best Fae court curtsy—my muscles screaming. I guess those queen lessons were paying off.

"Yes, your majesty."

Her gaze lit on her son's face, and her eyes narrowed to serpent slits. *What have you done to my son?* Her mental voice arrowed through my brain, and I flinched.

Well, shit. She was going to eat us. I was sure of it. The sweat started to pool in the curve of my lower back, even though it was chilly. I wiped drops of perspiration from my brow.

I did it myself, Goch said, his tone repentant. *I didn't listen and got into some trouble. Mr. Mittens saved me.*

Who is this Mr. Mittens? she demanded.

Goch was quiet, so I said quietly, "My cat."

Cat? She sent a mental image of a lion, and I sent one back of my fluffy Ragdoll. She recoiled. *How can such a thing save a dragon? We could end one with a snap of our teeth, or a swat of our talons!*

"He's not what he appears," I added quickly and sent another image of his true form, and one that showed him shapeshifting. Her posture relaxed, and she huffed. A stream of smoke poured from her nostrils. I took an involuntary step back. I had to; instinct told me to flee the scary beast. I swallowed hard.

She scowled at Goch, examining the claw marks, now scarred over, and his broken horn.

The horn will not grow back. How could you be so careless? It'll make battling for a mate more difficult.

Huh, I guess that's why the males grew horns. Go figure.

Mr. Mittens is training me to fight, I'm fierce! Goch insisted.

He was? When? Seriously, my cat had a whole secret life where he was uncle to griffin chicks and had a whole warrior training class thing going. Plus, he helped Megan as well. I shook my head. He was an incredible fighter, though; I was sure he could teach the dragon a few things.

Hmmm. She turned her focus back to us. *What is it you wish to ask?* Her good mood had soured, and with it, my hopes. I felt myself deflating, already defeated. At least I didn't feel like she would eat us now, just turn us down.

"Umm, Goch told us about the dragon collar that allows you to concentrate magic. We wish to borrow it for a short time."

Her gaze narrowed to Goch, and it was clear they were conversing silently. Megan and I moved to the side. The intensity of the immense creatures was difficult to stand between. Everything in our beings was yelling at us to run or hide. We were both visibly trembling with fear we couldn't control. Like our lizard brains knew that some-where in human history, dragons had hunted us.

I watched Goch to see if I could read him. He cowered a bit, then straightened and looked angry. Then he settled to sulky. Damn. This wasn't going well.

Finally, he sat up tall, defiant. The queen's eyes and the weight of her gaze settled back on me.

My son is mistaken. He should have paid more attention to dragon lore in school. It is true the Golden Collar of Merlin is a great treasure to us, but it hasn't worked for many hundreds of years. I'm very sorry it will not help you.

My heart sank. I didn't think I'd put much hope in this artifact, but at the same time, I must have. I turned to leave. Megan's eyes showed her disappointment as well when they met mine.

Wait, mother! Goch projected so hard his mental voice echoed in my skull. *Brigid is a great enchanter like Merlin was. She can make it work again; I know it! Let her borrow it, fix it, use it, and when she returns it, our most treasured artifact will be great again!*

I staggered, astounded that he thought of me as capable. I wasn't a "great enchanter;" I was still a beginner. I turned back to the queen, an idea forming. I wasn't great, but I knew great magic users. I bet Dana could fix it. In fact, the surety started burning in my breast like a sun.

"I'd be honored to be allowed to try," I managed to squeak out.

Megan tugged on my arm and whispered, "What are you doing?"

"I have an idea." I brushed off her hand.

"If it's Dana, don't bet on it."

"It is, and I think she might be able to."

She sighed. "Weak."

"You have any other ideas?" I hissed back.

"No. But not pissing off the dragons is a great way to start."

I rolled my eyes.

The queen peered at me, her face coming dangerously close. *If you can do such a thing, the dragons will be forever grateful and consider you a friend.*

I gulped, but I made myself ask, "What if I cannot fix it?"

Her head snapped back, making me dizzy. *The council of elders will decide your fate. They are not fond of non-dragons.*

I didn't know what that meant, but it sounded serious. I'd better succeed. Or in this case, Dana better.

I nodded my head but added, "I'll try."

She was quiet for a moment, staring at me. *It will be so.* She lifted her head, turning her face toward the ceiling, and let out a piercing call. The three dragons that had escorted us earlier entered the cavern.

She spoke into our minds, so we'd hear her commands this time. *Escort them to the hoard, and inform the elders to release the Golden Collar of Merlin to this human.*

The dragons appeared surprised, and the amethyst colored one glared at us, but they didn't argue.

We mounted Goch and laid down for launch. It was a much gentler lurch, since we weren't trying to rise quickly over trees. Soon enough we burst through the gigantic cavern into the daylight.

The occasional sunbeam bouncing off the brilliant dragon scales as we flew around the peaks blinded us, and I mentally added tinted ski goggles to my shopping list, and something for our hair, aviator caps? I didn't know. I made a mental note to ask Megan what they used on Pern; I didn't remember.

I shrugged. I was now thinking Pern was real as well. Dumb. Oh well, using the novels as a manual had helped us so far. Ann McCaffrey must have known the local Irish dragons.

Goch banked hard and took us through a tight canyon. He was larger than the other three, and his wingtips looked as though they'd score the rock face we passed through. We made it, barely. My heart beat fast, pounding hard against my breastbone. He was a creature of the air; I shouldn't worry while I was on his back.

We raced through a few more canyons and then faced the largest mountain on the island. I didn't see a cave as I scanned the area. We continued to fly directly at the cliff face. I gulped. We were going to ram into it directly! I felt the scream build in my throat, and I closed my eyes tightly, anticipating pain and death. Instead, a cool darkness descended. I opened my eyes into the dimness of a new, immense cavern.

Sorry, Megan and Brigid. I couldn't warn you, I had to concentrate on the code so we could pass through the illusion that guards the cave of the hoard. It is strong, and if you don't concentrate, it won't let you through. He did sound apologetic, but it wasn't that big of a deal—a moment of intense fear, then it passed.

We continued following the trio of dragons. Although the initial cavern was nearly as large as the queen's, this one had many tight turns and narrow passages we had to wind our way through. In several, we had to go single file, and I wondered how any dragon larger than Goch could make the tight corridors when flying.

We flew for a long time. I didn't know how far, but deep into the interior of the mountain. The weight of the rock above us pressed down on my psyche. I found myself gasping for air, although other than the smell of minerals and water, the air was clear and clean. We slowed, and the three dragons in front of us suddenly disappeared. I gasped.

Hold on, Goch said.

I clutched the harness tighter. My stomach dropped, and I felt weightless as Goch dove straight down.

Chapter Eight

I couldn't help it, I screamed. Megan did too. We literally dove down a hole and hurtled for what felt like miles. The harness tightened painfully over my thighs as the sharp angle tried to rip us free. Goch's wings were tight on his sides, and we huddled low on his back. The walls of the volcanic tube felt so tight I thought we might be scraped off his back at any moment.

It was pitch black, and I called my light magic out and hung it above us as we plummeted. Even with the light, we couldn't see where we were going, the hole was too deep, and the walls too narrow for the light to pass froward and illuminate the way, although the dragons weren't concerned.

Suddenly, the space around us expanded, and Goch snapped his wings open. The movement slammed us back and was nearly painful, but the relief overcame the pain. We slowed and turned along another corridor. It grew steadily larger until we could fly in formation again.

We approach the hoard, Goch announced, and I took a breath. I guess I'd been holding it for a while.

My lungs were starved for air, and I gulped it down. I increased the intensity of my light, and as we burst through the tunnel into the next cavern, the sparkle of gold and gems took my breath away.

This was the main chamber of an ancient volcano. Above us, perhaps a mile or more was a gleam of sky. I looked over the cavern. Who knew how deep the hoard was. It looked like something you'd see in a pirate treasure chest, just on an unbelievable scale. Everything glittered. My light bounced off gold, silver, gems, and stuff I couldn't identify; a true hoard of unbelievable wealth filled the old volcano. Once I tore my eyes away from it, I glanced about and finally noticed the dragons that sat on ledges ringing the entire space. Their eyes glowed slightly, and I dimmed my light again so I didn't annoy them.

Goch backwinged, and without a place to land, he settled on the hoard itself, his talons tinkling off of gold coins and other metallic objects. The three dragons that had escorted us, flew a circle around the hoard at eye level of the guardian dragons, and then left the same way we'd come. I wondered why they didn't just go straight up, but perhaps the opening wasn't large enough. It was hard to tell from this far below.

Why do you disturb us and bring strangers to the hoard, child? A feminine voice rang in my brain.

I am here under the protection of Queen Aurora Golden Scales, Goch announced. *And these humans have her permission to borrow one of our greatest treasures.*

There was a loud hiss from the dragons ringing the hoard, the sound primal and angry. I shuddered.

This is Brigid, enchantress of the humans, and she is going to repair one of our greatest treasures, the Golden Collar of Merlin, he continued.

I wished I hadn't promised that. It was a weak promise I wasn't sure I could deliver. Oh well, the worst-case scenario was I couldn't do it, and the vamps would kill me before the dragons had their chance.

I sat straighter and tried to look confident.

The queen oversteps herself! A different voice, male, zinged through my head. *The elders decide how the hoard is used!*

Anxiety shot through me. What if they didn't let us have it after all?

Another extended hiss. *No one but an elder dragon has ever touched the collar. Why should we give it to you, human?* Yet a different voice said.

I cleared my throat, and although I spoke out loud, I tried to reinforce it mentally as I sent my words to the elders.

"I am a friend to dragons. I accepted Goch and supplied him with a teacher to learn to realm walk and fight…" That was a stretch, but Mr. Mittens would go along if asked. "I have need of the collar, so that I might fight the vampires that infest my land. Goch suggested it, although we were unaware that it was broken. I do have some skill and believe I may be able to fix it if given the chance." I looked around and reached in to grab my gift. "I've brought a gift. An object of such great enchantment it can cure anything from the smallest to even the greatest of ills." I held up one of Dana's magic healing balls. "It has brought back several from the brink of death."

I waited. Megan looked at me over her shoulder and gave me a thumbs up. I wondered if we should dismount, but Goch hadn't said anything. And if we needed to leave fast, it made sense to stay on his back.

The dragons appeared to converse, although it wasn't out loud, but their heads swung back and forth looking at each other.

Finally, once my nerves were about to fray completely, a massive red dragon, like Goch, fluttered down onto the hoard and approached us.

Goch inclined his head, and we followed the gesture.

I am Darg, consort to the late Galanthea Golden Fire, grandsire of Goch. The elders have decided. We will allow you to take the Golden Collar of Merlin for one fortnight under the condition that you repair it. If you do not, you will face our judgment. He glanced at Goch, who was still looking down. *As will my grandson. If you agree, you will leave with the collar.*

I swallowed, but I'd already made the decision. I reached out to Goch. He hadn't known this would reflect back on him. "Are you sure?"

There was a moment, and I wondered if he regretted this. *I'm sure, Brigid. I have faith in you.*

That nearly broke me.

I pushed it aside and answered, "I agree." I straightened my spine and decided to panic after we returned home.

I gave the dragon the magic ball, and he took it tenderly in his talons. I sent him a mental image of how it was used, and he set it carefully in the hoard. I blinked. How would they find it if it was needed? I shook my head.

The red dragon rose to his great height and opened his wings, taking the rampart position. An object rose from the hoard and hovered before him. Ah, telekinesis. They could manipulate whatever they wished in the hoard. He settled back in the gold pile, and the collar floated towards me. It was large, and I could see it slipping easily over a dragon's head to lie at the base of its long neck against the body.

Before it reached me, it shrunk in size, until it looked

like one of those ancient Egyptian necklace bands that also sat at the base of the neck. In the center of the chevron shaped middle was the largest cut ruby I'd ever seen.

It seemed to catch any light and glow with power. The collar landed in my hands, and a tingle of magic shot up my arm. It felt like Fae magic.

I must have sat there staring at it a while, because Megan whispered, "Are you OK?"

I snapped out of it. I put the collar on over my head, and it settled over my collar bone, fitting itself as though it had been made for me.

"Yeah, we'll talk later."

The red dragon looked as though he was going to spring away.

I had questions. "Did you know Merlin? Was he Fae?"

The dragon swung his head back to me. *I did. He was born on this planet, but I do believe he was half Fae.*

That explained the familiar tingle of magic surrounding the collar.

"Is he dead?" I asked.

The dragon cocked his head at me. *I do not know. He left long ago, and I do not know where.*

"Oh. Thank you."

The dragon didn't respond; he just leapt up, golden coins raining down from his claws, and returned to his perch along the walls.

Leave us. The elder dragons demanded. We didn't dare wait. His command was hard to resist. We positioned ourselves for takeoff, and Goch leapt up.

Chapter Nine

I expected Goch to weave us back out of the cavern, but instead, the pulse of realm walking magic zapped through me, and we were on the Fae practice planet, and seconds later, we spiraled lazily over the woods of home. I took a deep breath.

Now, I had the potential of vamp attacks, a griffin war, and the new possibility that the dragons would come for me as well. From the frying pan into the fire. If I let myself dwell on it, I would probably curl into the fetal position and suck my thumb.

Goch landed in the parking lot, and we unclipped and slid off. My back was sore. Dragon riding took a whole different set of muscles than riding horseback. It was hard on the spine, and my legs were Jell-O. Plus, a cushion for my bony butt would be nice for another long jaunt if I ever did it again.

Megan was rubbing her butt as well, and since she had a nice round one, I didn't feel as bad.

"I'm getting a cushion," she mumbled.

I laughed. "I was just thinking the same thing."

"Well, bony dragon back isn't very comfortable."

I nodded. She reached over and touched the jewel in the center of the collar.

"Is the jewel the amulet, or the whole thing?" she asked.

I shrugged. "No idea."

She circled me, her hands running around the collar. "How do you take it off? There's no latch?"

I reached up and felt the whole thing with my fingers. I tried to take it off over my head, but the opening was too small. I started to panic. How would I fix it or give it back if I couldn't take it off? Plus, how would Dana examine it? I took a deep breath. I was too tired to deal with it right now. I just wanted to soak in my tub, eat ice cream, and go to bed.

Instead, I had a text from Jim. *"New mare is here. Can you come by?"*

I sighed. "Megan, you feel like a walk to the dairy?"

She stretched, hands on her back. "Sure, I need to walk out these sore muscles. What's up?"

"I'm not sure."

Just then, Mr. Mittens came trotting out the back door. He meowed at us. *You were gone a long time,* he said. *I was concerned.* He looked me, Megan, and Goch over. *You appear to have survived.*

I bent over and gave him head scritches. "We did. Although, we might not be around in two weeks when we need to return this thing if I can't even get it off my neck."

Yes. That is troublesome. He gazed at the collar.

We walked through the trees towards the dairy.

It has an aura of Fae magic, he said, his blue-eyed gaze piercing me.

"It feels like that to me as well. It appears that our enchanter, Merlin, was part Fae. I'm hoping that Dana or my grandfather can help us reactivate or fix it or whatever."

Hmpf. If not, you can. You are powerful.

"I know I am, but I don't know how to use it." Even I could hear the frustration in my voice.

We opened the gate into the first field. A streak of gold rocketed by us. Then the little foal galloped up and thrust his tiny muzzle into my belly.

"Milk Dud! How are you?" I stroked the unicorn foal's soft ears and muzzle and rubbed the little nub of a horn. It always seemed itchy.

He whinnied. Then he tossed his head and galloped away. We followed him through to the next pasture. Jim stood at the fence, his arms resting along the top, leaning in and watching. I noticed the mare then. She was a healthy-looking sorrel but stood in the field with her head down, not grazing. She looked sad.

We joined him on the opposite side of the fence. "What's wrong with her?" I asked, tilting my head towards the mare.

"I think she's depressed. She lost her foal, that's why we bought her here, to see if she would accept the unicorn."

"He ran up to us, have they interacted at all?"

"Not yet. He ran off when I put him in the field. I'm sure he'll be right back, just feeling his oats."

A moment later, Milk Dud ran back up to the fence and snorted at us, shaking his short, upright mane.

"Hey, buddy," Jim said.

I went over to the mare and tugged on her halter; she responded easily and plodded over to the fence with me. Her ears pricked forward at the tiny foal. The unicorn snorted gently and leaned his muzzle towards her. They breathed into each other's nostrils, then she sniffed down his neck. The foal gamboled around, bucking, but sidled back up to her.

She knickered low in her throat. Her eyes soft.

"I think she'll accept him," I muttered to Jim.

He nodded. The foal bumped her side with his muzzle, and she guided him back to her udder. He butted her again, then latched on and started to suckle. We all held our breath.

Then we let ourselves out of the enclosure quietly to avoid startling the pair. We stood and watched the magic of a gentle mother. Her head came up, and there was a new light in her eyes.

"Well, that's a relief," Jim said. "Bottle feeding him has become a handful. She'll handle him better than I can."

I felt guilty. I'd sort of dumped the problem in his lap. "Sorry Jim, I should have helped more."

"It's my job. Besides, I like the little beast." He looked at the little critter fondly.

We'd also never bothered changing his name, so it looked like we were stuck with Milk Dud. It was a stupid name for a unicorn, but there it was. Maybe the candy sweetness would wear off on him, and he wouldn't grow up to be a huge dick like the rest of his race.

"How is the hamburger supplement?" Unicorns ate meat, and since it was our first time raising one, we'd been experimenting on the best feed for him.

"He nibbles on it, but still mostly drinks milk. He's still small, most horse foals can be weaned after four months, so he's got a few months to go."

I nodded. "He looks healthy, so I guess what we're doing is working." I looked around. Since we were here, I should check in on the baincapall. After we'd lost two of

Sorcha's soldiers to the vamps, she'd been running a tighter ship.

"Thanks, Jim. This looks like a win. I'm gonna go check on the baincapall crew."

He nodded.

Megan, Mr. Mittens, and I peeled off and headed to the barracks. I knocked before entering. They rotated shifts, so I didn't know who would be off shift and available to chat. I tried to check in daily, although it didn't always work out.

We walked in. Luckily, Sorcha was off shift today and lounging on an oversized beanbag in front of the TV. I looked up and saw she was watching a war movie. I snorted a laugh. Of course, always training or thinking about new techniques.

"Hey, Sorcha! How is everything going?"

She hit pause. Since being here, she'd become quite adept at earth tech. She even texted me now.

"Quiet." She peeled her seven-foot frame off the beanbag and stood. "There hasn't been a single vampire sighting, but a few strange creatures that attacked us have been put down."

Incursions, Mr. Mittens huffed.

That was usually his job, but he had so many now, it was hard to keep up with the one he'd been doing for over a century.

She shrugged. "They give my soldiers extra training, keeps them alert."

"Do you need anything, or is all well?" I asked.

"We have what we need."

Megan moved to my right side. "I've been practicing that move you showed me, can I join training tomorrow?"

Sorcha blinked and frowned, "You should come every morning."

"I train with Dana as well, so I can't always come, but she is busy a lot, so if you don't mind, I'll join you on the days she doesn't show."

Wow, Megan had really turned into a warrior. I wasn't sure if I was sad that being my friend had done this to her or proud of her fierceness. I leaned towards proud. Both of us had better lives than we had before I'd left my cheating ex and bought the B&B.

Sorcha noticed the collar around my neck, because I saw her gaze catch it and stick.

"Where did you get that?" she asked.

Which was odd. She'd never noticed what I wore.

"I just retrieved it from the dragons."

"That is the Golden Collar of Merlin," she said, pointing at it, her face set in a deep frown. She took an aggressive step forward, her body tense, her focus on the collar.

Shock frissoned through me. I'd never heard of this thing, but Sorcha, a Fae centaur, had? My hand reached up and touched it. The cool metal outside of the collar was smooth under my fingers. "Yeah, how did you know that?"

She stopped, checking herself. I could see the warring emotions run across her face. "It was stolen many, many years ago. One of our missions is to seek it when we are off duty. It's become a joke, because no one knows where it went. How did you get it?"

She sounded more accusatory than friendly at the moment, and I reached up to defensively grab the collar again.

Mr. Mittens growled a warning.

"I asked to borrow it. It is a great treasure to the dragons. They claim Merlin made it for them."

"They lie."

Chapter Ten

That startled me, and I took a step back. The dragons hadn't appeared to lie. They held the collar in great regard. I'd believed the story utterly.

She crossed her arms, but she was still agitated. "Merlin made it for the wedding of the summer queen, many hundreds of years ago. It disappeared before the wedding. It was said to contain great power." Her eyes hadn't left the collar.

I clutched the cold metal. What was the truth? Would it be safe to deliver it to Faerie to have Dana look at it? If Sorcha reacted to it this way, what would others who didn't know me do? I couldn't lose it; the dragons would destroy us in moments.

"Well, it's theirs now, and I'm bound to return it in a fortnight. The Fae court will have to take it up with the dragons," I said defensively.

She finally tore her gaze away, her tension draining. Mr. Mittens stopped growling but continued to watch the warrior. I had no doubt he'd tear her to pieces before she could move against me, but she was my friend.

"It's OK, Mr. Mittens. She's my friend; she won't hurt me."

Hmpf, I know that look in her eyes.

"Are we going to have a problem over this?" I asked.

She stiffened. "No, that is not my current mission. However, now I know where it is, I'll have to take it back eventually, but I'll deal with the dragons, not you, my friend." Her demeanor returned to her earlier languor.

I felt a chill of foreboding slide down my spine. A dangerous magical artifact with ancient provenance and ties to Merlin, who was apparently known on more than one world, didn't make me feel safe. I needed to get this thing off, figured out, used, and returned as soon as possible.

"Well, it doesn't work, currently, that's one of my tasks. Then, I'm gonna use it to take the fight to the vamps."

She nodded and went over to the refrigerator, taking out an energy drink. She popped the top and slammed it back.

I looked at Megan, who looked back at me and shrugged. An Amazonian-sized female warrior centaur hopped up on sugar and caffeine seemed like a bad idea. I shivered. Glad she was on our side.

"Text me if you need anything," I said. "We're heading out."

She waved, crushed the can, and tossed it into the recycle bin. "I will."

We turned and left. I had to get this collar off, now, before someone decided it would be easier to retrieve it by removing my head first.

Milk Dud was done nursing, but he leaned against the mare, who kept checking to make sure he was there. They both were lonely. I hoped they were happy with each other

—mother and foal. I scrubbed her forehead with my hand and thanked her quietly. She didn't understand, but it made me feel like I'd been instrumental in one good deed today.

Milk Dud was drowsy, so I didn't pet him on the way out. Mr. Mittens was still wary around him—or guilty, I wasn't sure which. The foal was too small to be a danger to us, and his horn and fire wouldn't manifest until long after he was weaned, so maybe it was guilt that he'd killed its mother. I didn't know.

We were all hoping that nurture beat nature with the little beast. He was pretty accepting of us all so far. But he depended on us for everything, so who knew.

We passed through the last gate and hurried towards the house. It was growing dark and had started to drizzle. It was a temperate rainforest, and rain was expected more often than sunlight, I reminded myself before I grew too annoyed at it.

We cleared the trees and began to walk across the parking lot to the house, when a swarm of bats flittered overhead. Mr. Mittens leapt up, much further than a typical domestic cat, and swatted one out of the air.

My breath caught, and Megan had her sword out faster than I could blink and pierced it through the heart. Nothing happened. Mr. Mittens glared at her.

Hmpf. They are regular bats. I felt like a snack.

I laughed, the adrenaline hitting my system, and the bats fluttered away. Only, something fell from the sky. My heart clenched again, and my hand trembled as I picked up the heavy cream envelope from the ground. Only one person I knew sent things like this. Vic Constantine, the vampire Vendetta leader himself.

Megan's sword disappeared back into its ball and into

her pocket. "Is that a letter from the vamps?" she asked, recognizing the letter as well.

"I think so, we'll see inside." I scanned the area around us, as did Mr. Mittens, but he didn't transform, so I assumed the danger had left on bat wings.

We climbed the few steps to the back porch and entered through the kitchen door. Chef Jack had dinner prepared. Gabe was scrolling through his phone when we walked in. His smile lit up the room.

I kissed him and sat next to him at the heavy oak table. I showed him the envelope, and he froze. My hand trembled. What fresh hell awaited us inside? I leaned against Gabe. His arms reached around my waist in support. I took a deep breath and opened it.

"*Dear Ms. Donovan,*" it began. "*I do appreciate you returning my wife to me. In gratitude, I've decided to grant you another parley. We can meet as we did before. Please respond with a date so we may resume hostilities in a timely fashion. Yours, Ludovic Constantine.*"

I flipped it over, nothing else was written. What a weird letter. I had nothing to say to him, what would be the benefit of a parley? He still was planning to continue "hostilities."

"Is he delusional?" Megan threw up her hands.

"He's something, for sure," I handed the letter to Gabe.

He looked it over. "He's screwing with us."

Something was certainly weird. I couldn't put my finger on what though. Was he trying to lure me out into a trap? Was he sincere? Since he called for a parley, was he going to offer terms to end this war? I didn't know, and I definitely didn't trust him. There was no way I was going anywhere until I had the collar working properly. To do that, I needed Dana.

Megan and I explained everything that had happened

with the dragons and the problem with the amulet. Gabe also examined it and couldn't figure out how to remove it.

"I'm going to call Dana," I announced. I'd given my grandfather and Dana each a phone that would work on magic so we could talk to one another. I pulled out my phone and opened my contacts. I swiped to "Dana" and hit call. This was the first time I'd called from this realm. I put the phone to my ear and listened to the normal ring tone.

I'd shown Dana how to use the phone, but that had been only one time. I wondered if she carried it around or if she left it somewhere when she was busy. Since she didn't answer, she either didn't remember how to or had left it behind. Frustrating.

"She didn't answer," I said, although both Megan and Gabe could guess that from my actions. "I guess I'm going on a trip to Faerie."

I looked at my cat and the two humans. "Anyone fancy a trip?"

Gabe shook his head. "I'm working so I don't dare go." That wasn't a surprise; he hadn't made it yet.

"I'm game," Megan said.

I go where you go, Mr. Mittens said.

"Thank you." I scratched behind his ears, and he leaned into my hand.

"Tomorrow is soon enough, I'm exhausted," I announced.

"Yeah, me too," Megan added.

We ate our dinner, and after, I settled into the crook of Gabe's arm in the bed.

"I have a surprise delivery tomorrow. Can you take care of it? You'll need to ask Luke or someone to help you."

He raised an eyebrow. "What is it?"

"Well, since the bed is now too small for three, I ordered a bigger one."

"There's something bigger than this?" he asked.

"Yeah, do you remember that old John Denver song, 'Grandma's Feather Bed?'"

He scrunched up his face, thinking. "I think so."

"Well, that's what's coming." I laughed. It was actually bigger.

Chapter Eleven

The bed was delivered early. Like that *ever* happened. Mr. Mittens cocked his head at me.

"I solved the issue. You don't have to move your bed now."

He rubbed against my legs, almost knocking me down.

Thank you, Brigid. His voice was bright and happy in my mind.

He didn't often lay in it or sleep all night; cats were mostly nocturnal—even alien cats, apparently. I leaned down and scratched his head. "I love you Mr. Mittens, I gave you your bed and its place of honor. I wasn't going to take that back from you."

That earned me a loud purr. I petted him and stood.

The collar was still around my neck. Sleeping hadn't done anything to dislodge it, it was horribly uncomfortable, and no one had any ideas on how to remove it without damaging it. Gabe had left for work early, so I had the delivery men set up the bed—Gabe was off the hook. My old king-sized bed was still fairly new, so I had them place it out of the way in my personal drawing room, I'd worry about it later.

Our bedroom was large and included the round curve of the three-story tall turret. However, after placing my nine-foot square bed, it finally seemed more *proportionate*. I no longer had a headboard, but if I missed it, I supposed I could have one made to fit. I closed and locked my door. Megan was sitting in the kitchen eating a delicious Chef Jack breakfast, so I joined her after I fed my cat a premium meal of salmon.

Mr. Mittens was in an excellent mood. As soon as he took a deer to Brightfeather, we were going to leave for Faerie. Megan and I were dressed in our Faerie robes, the golden collar with the huge ruby stood out against my blue dress. Too bad I wanted the amulet off; it looked magnificent when I admired it in the mirror.

I kept reaching up and tugging on it, which was making the skin around my throat raw and irritated. Plus, the magic that surrounded it was like a low vibration just at the edge of sound that was growing more and more annoying.

It had to come off. It just had to.

Mr. Mittens finished his meal and drifted out the door. I still wasn't sure how he did it. I hadn't felt the pulse of realm walking magic; it was like matter just obeyed him when he wanted in or out of somewhere.

"I wonder if I should take another gift to Dana."

Megan shrugged. "Everyone likes a gift."

I didn't have anything unless she wanted a lightly used king-sized bed. Then I had an idea. Since she loved earth pastries, and we had to wait for Mr. Mittens to return after delivering the deer to Brightfeather, I asked Chef Jack what he could have prepared in an hour.

He said he'd surprise me.

I texted Jim about the unicorn foal. He said everything was still working out, and mother and foal were happy. We had nothing left to do but wait for the pastries and Mr. Mittens before we left for Faerie.

—————

An hour later, we realm walked to my grandfather's keep—a large bakery box full of homemade cinnamon rolls in my hands. My grandfather didn't appear to be home, but Dana was ensconced in her lab. She looked at me suspiciously when I handed her the large pink box.

She sniffed it once and set it on a semi-cleared table. "What is it you seek?" Her hand zipped into the box and pulled out a delectable treat, still warm from the oven.

"It's a long story, and we don't know if you'll even be able to help us," I started, hoping she'd be determined to help after an introduction like that.

The first roll disappeared. Dana licked her extra-long green fingers with her long pointed tongue. I had to keep myself from shuddering.

"It started when we found out about an artifact that could help with my power issue off the land."

Dana was well aware of it, since she'd been trying to come up with something portable for us. Her eyes sharpened with interest, and she lifted a second roll to her mouth.

"I'll leave out the details, but this thing around my throat is the answer. It's called the Golden Collar of Merlin."

She dropped the roll and stared. She swallowed. "That's impossible."

I shook my head. "No, it's been on earth. Apparently, Merlin made it for the dragons."

"No, that's a lie."

That was exactly what Sorcha had said and why I was nervous about coming here.

"Yeah, I heard that from one of the baincapall—something about a wedding gift for a queen?"

Dana tapped a long finger against her chin thoughtfully. Her black shark eyes drifting back to the collar. "Yes, it disappeared before the wedding. Lots of accusations flew, there were arrests, fighting, war. In fact, it led to the dissolution of the summer, winter, autumn, and spring courts."

I swallowed. Well, crap.

"I can't give it back to the Fae, I had to agree to return it in two weeks to the dragons. But it doesn't work. I need it to work. We were hoping you could fix it."

She flicked her long fingers towards the collar in dismissal. "I don't care about the artifact, but don't let anyone else see it."

I looked at Megan, who was silently trying to give me advice on what to say. It was basically a bunch of awkward facial gestures and mouthing words I couldn't make out. I shook my head slightly, then turned back to Dana. "Well, there's another problem. It won't come off."

Dana's glance sharpened, and her gaze once again focused on the collar. She picked up her dropped treat and munched thoughtfully. After a few bites, she said. "It's magic. Ask it to open with your power."

I wanted to say, "how the hell do I do that?" but I didn't want Dana to strike me dead. I didn't know what she meant or how to do it.

I grasped the collar with my hand, and said, "Open?"

Nothing happened. Dana rolled her eyes. "With your

power," she repeated, like saying it again would make me understand this time.

I sighed. "I don't know what that means."

She shrugged and continued munching.

I thought about it this time, pushing power into it. *Open!*

This time, the collar grew, and I was able to slip it over my head. I breathed a sigh of relief. Dana held out her now empty hand and took the collar, examining it carefully.

She handed it back to me.

"It doesn't appear broken."

I wanted to huff out in frustration. "It isn't doing what it's supposed to do."

"What is it supposed to do?"

"Harness energy or magic or something, so it can be retrieved."

"Are you sure?"

Megan leaned on one of the many tables, watching us like a tennis match. Mr. Mittens rubbed against my legs, avoiding Dana's notice. He was positive she detested him. Since I was kinda sure she felt the same way about me, I didn't blame him for avoiding her.

"We aren't sure. We only know what the dragons told us," Megan volunteered. "But it used to do something, and no one can make it do anything now."

"Hmmm."

I handed it back to her. She touched the stone, and I could feel a tiny spark of magic. She sat it on her worktable, the rolls forgotten. She grabbed a tool and started jabbing at the jewel, it looked like she was trying to dislodge it from its setting. A little bolt of electricity zapped her, and she dropped her tool. She glared at the collar.

This time, she held her hands over it, and I could feel magic building in the room. She muttered some words I couldn't understand, and the magic grew. She released a golden rush of magic at the jewel. It glowed blue, the light building until it was blinding white. Then it pulsed once, and Dana staggered back.

She looked confused and annoyed. She tried again. The results varied, so she continued to try, but other than Dana growing more frustrated, nothing else happened.

"Leave it with me, I have more things to try, but it's dangerous."

I looked at Megan, and Mr. Mittens pressed harder against me. We left the room.

Chapter Twelve

"That didn't look good," Megan said, pointing back the way we'd come.

We walked slowly away from the lab. I rubbed the raw patches on my neck. "I know. What am I going to do if she can't figure it out?"

Megan grabbed her skirts and fluffed them, trying to free her feet from the acres of fabric. She didn't look concerned. "Find Merlin." She shrugged and continued to fidget with her dress.

I stopped and turned to face her. "What? You can't be serious."

She finally just picked up the bottom hem and tucked it into the waistband, then casually said, "There's a good chance he's alive if he's Fae, right?"

Well, damn. "Maybe? But no one has seen him since King Arthur's time! He was supposed to be trapped by some Fae woman. Locked for eternity in a crystal cave? Something like that, I'm not up on the lore," I said as I kicked out my skirts. We weren't used to being in long gowns anymore.

"Well, we're in Faerie. We can ask around." She did a little scuffling step and thrust an imaginary sword at an imaginary opponent.

I stared at her. Hands on my hips. "Who? Who do we ask? We can't tell them about the collar. It's a big deal here, and I don't want anyone else to know I have it." I shuddered. "If someone took it from us, the dragons would fry me for sure."

She spun, did another air sword move, and then slammed it into her imaginary scabbard. "You have connections at court, why don't you ask your grandfather to talk to the king? Surely, he has a court researcher or something equivalent."

We started walking towards Grandfather's den. I sighed. "I guess."

We took a few steps. "What do you know about Merlin?" she asked.

I shrugged. "I don't know, the usual stuff. Arthur's advisor and magician. Why?"

"Uh, you need to read more. There's a lot of stuff, and most of it is contradictory. Like he was a boy at the same time as Arthur, and sometimes he's an old man. Some say he lived backwards, which is ridiculous, and some say he was just a crazy dude who sometimes had visions." She started stretching her arms, pulling one forward and across her body, then reaching it up over her head and rotating it in a circle.

"What does it matter? We know he was real, we know he was at least part Fae, and we know he built the collar." I was still too stiff from dragon riding to do anything more than walk.

She let both arms fall back to her sides. "Well, maybe there's a hint about where he ended up. Some say he fell in love with a Faerie woman named Nimue. She might have been the Lady of the Lake. I don't know for sure, because I can't remember. Anyway, in one of the stories, he teaches her all his magic, and she uses it to freeze him in a cave. Some say she killed him. But the only thing we know for sure, is he disappeared at that time. So, if he came back here, maybe he's with that Nimue lady. Right?"

"So, if we find her, we find him?"

She shrugged. "It gives us two people to look for, anyway."

I cocked my head at her and squinted. "So, you think finding two needles in a haystack will be easier than one?"

She laughed. "Maybe, you never know."

I sighed. "I'm screwed. We should start looking for land here; we can't go back."

"We have all the time we want." She pointed at me. "You can manipulate time."

I stopped in my tracks. I thought for a second. I couldn't really manipulate time, but I could go back and forth in it. "You're right. The only problem is, once I go home from here, I risk messing up my own timeline. We have time here, but not there."

She did a whole-body shudder. "Don't talk time travel; it messes with my head."

"You brought it up!" I shook my head. "It messes with mine, too. Trust me, I almost hate the ability."

"I'd hate it, too, if it hadn't saved our bacon more than once."

I shivered, remembering that according to my grandfather, I'd lost everyone I loved in an explosion. I'd used time travel to stop it, but that was too close for comfort.

We turned the last corner. Since my grandfather wasn't home, we went to his den to hang out until Dana was through with her experiments. Mr. Mittens didn't have much to contribute, since he didn't know Merlin and hadn't heard of him. He jumped up in one of the chairs and curled up in nap position.

Megan decided to spend time searching through the books that lined the walls of the room. Neither of us had had time to peruse them much before, other than a cursory look. I didn't even know if we could read them.

"Can you read those?" I asked, from the chair by the fire.

"Nah, but I wish I could."

"Come here, let's see if I can add the ability to the necklace." She hopped off the ladder. I grabbed the gem around her throat, closed my eyes, and willed it to allow her to read any language and pushed my magic into it. There was a brief flash of light.

"Is that it?"

"I think so, go try it!"

She went back and plucked a book from the shelf. There weren't any titles on the spines, so she opened it. "A History of Warfare," she read aloud.

"Damn, it worked!" I said, surprised and excited. I smiled. Maybe I could become an enchanter, maybe it was just a matter of *willing* what I wanted to happen.

I was wearing my engagement ring, so I did the same spell on it and started looking through random books.

"Do you think your grandfather has anything on Merlin in here?" Megan asked as she opened and closed a few books and put them back.

I shrugged. "I don't know, but since so few of these have titles, it'll take forever to look through them."

"Your wealthy, powerful grandfather probably has people that can tell us. Where's the steward guy?"

"Pull the rope."

She hopped off the ladder, walked to the fireplace, and pulled the silken cord that hung there, summoning the help.

We continued to pluck random books and glance in them while we waited. It didn't take long, my grandfather had excellent servants, and most of the time you didn't even notice them. The steward entered wearing my grandfather's livery. "How may I help you?" He gave us a stiff formal bow.

"Well, we were wondering, is there a catalog of the books, or someone that can tell us what's in the library?" I asked him.

He bowed his head. "There is indeed. Shall I summon him?"

"Oh, yes, th…" I almost thanked him. "I ap-preciate that." I stuttered out.

He gave another short bow and turned to leave.

It wasn't that much longer before he returned with a small man. I realized this was another goblin. My grandfather had a spymaster who was a goblin. The small stature, round eyes, crazy hair that looked like it was the texture of dandelion fluff, and wizened features were distinctive to the race.

"This is Flinter Carasis, the librarian." He bowed and left. I was a bit taken aback. Why had I been given his name? That wasn't a thing that was generally done in Faerie.

"Flint is fine," the goblin said in a squeaky voice.

"Can you tell us if there are any books here on Merlin?"

"Myrddin?"

I looked at Megan and whispered, "I think I've heard that before."

She nodded.

"Yes."

He tapped his temple with a long finger. "Yes, there are a few. I'll retrieve them."

I expected him to climb the ladder and slide along the wall, but he used magic to pull three large tomes from the shelves. The books settled on the large wooden table, where my grandfather looked at maps or threw his armor when he was annoyed at it.

"Do you require other books?" he squeaked, earnest to serve.

"Yeah, if you don't mind, is there anything on magical artifacts and how to construct them?" It couldn't hurt if Dana needed something to help her with the collar.

He pulled several more books down. I bowed in thanks and dismissed him. He told us how to summon him if we needed him, and he left.

Megan sat at the library table and pulled a random book towards her. I did the same. After the third book, my eyes were crossed, and I wished that Faerie had their own version of Google.

Megan must have felt the same, because she suddenly slammed a book shut and exasperatedly said, "Can't you just do a spell to show us what we want?"

I frowned at her. "I don't know. I mean, I've done it to find books before…" I'd used it to locate my grandmother's journals in the attic, but I hadn't done anything more fine-tuned than finding the books themselves.

"You limit yourself," Megan said, grumpily. "You are like one of the most powerful people in Faerie, and you act like you can't do anything."

She must be hungry or something. She usually didn't grouse at me unless she was. I closed my eyes and rubbed my neck. Then, I gathered up my magic, which came so easily in Faerie, and thought of what I wanted. I wanted information on the Collar of Merlin, and I pushed it out at the books on the table.

I opened my eyes. Megan was blinking. "That was bright."

There was often a flash of light if a spell worked. I scanned the books. Nothing. However, one book flew off the shelf and landed open on the table.

Chapter Thirteen

"Bingo," Megan said, leaning over the book. "Ha! It's here, look!" She pointed to a passage. Then she pulled her hair back and held it with one hand while she leaned over the book. I waited; the book wasn't big enough for two heads to lean over it.

"Ha!" she said again, but then kept reading. I was growing anxious about what she found.

"Well?"

She pointed to a passage. "It confirms the story about the queen and the wedding. But this appears to have been written by Merlin himself." Her finger traced down the page as she spoke. "He tells what really happened. The golden collar was going to be a wedding gift, but the prince who commissioned it for the wedding never paid for it, so Merlin kept it. The dragons offered an appropriate payment, so he sold it to them. It does belong to the dragons!" She slapped her hand on the book triumphantly.

That must have been her "ha" moment. "Anything about what it's supposed to do?"

"Not yet, there's a lot here about it, this'll take a minute."

That was frustrating. I didn't want to wait. "I'll just find something else."

I reached out with my magic and willed it to find anything that would show where Merlin was now. A book on the table fluttered but lay still. That wasn't very encouraging. I slid it towards me. Since it was the only response, I picked it up, sat by the fireplace, and scanned through it.

"Myrddin also known as Merlin, Emrys, or Ambrosius, came back to Faerie, following his..." I looked up at Megan. I was right; he had returned. I was about to tell her, but she was too engrossed in her book. I looked back down and searched for where he might have gone when he arrived here.

I continued to read. "He couldn't return to the Summer Court, after all, they were now involved in a war, and they were still annoyed at the debacle with the Golden Collar." I scanned further down for a town name or something.

"He was still under the protection of his lover, Nimue of the Autumn Court. Although she wasn't a royal member, she was high up in the court elite." Where was the Autumn Court? I scanned, my finger skimming the page. Damn. "The Autumn Court was eventually overrun, and Myrddin's location was lost. The last anyone heard of him was during the war. This author presumes that he is dead."

I slammed the book shut. Megan looked up at me with that long distance stare that told me she was entranced in her reading.

"What was that for?" she complained.

"I thought I had a lead on Merlin's location, but it was quite literally a dead end. The author said that he thought

Merlin was dead, ugh!" I slouched back in the chair. The book started to slide off my lap. I grabbed it.

"We might not need him after all," she said excitedly. "This has a lot of info on how the amulet was made, how to use it, and what it's for. We should get this to Dana, now."

"That's great." I heaved myself out of the chair and returned the book to the table. "What was the info?"

"Come on, I'll tell you as we walk back."

We left everything else on the table. I woke Mr. Mittens, who blinked sleepily at me. "We're going back to talk to Dana, do you want to come or stay?"

He yawned, showing his teeth—much longer and sharper than a domestic cat should have—and stretched out his front paw, the distinctive mitten standing out against the dark fabric of the chair. I thought for a moment he was going to stand, but he just sunk deeper into the chair. *I'll wait here.*

He didn't want to tangle with Dana, and he did look comfy.

I chuckled. "OK, see you soon."

We headed out the door and down the long winding corridor back to Dana's lab. Halfway there, a flash of light and the boom of an explosion rocked us. I bounced against the wall and fell against Megan. Clouds of smoke wafted towards us. We picked ourselves up and brushed ourselves off. We looked at each other and ran towards the lab.

The door had blown off, and scorch marks covered the wall. My heart pounded. Was Dana alright? Was she hurt? I scrambled over the door behind Megan. Dana was lying against the wall, partially propped up. From the dent in the wall and the smear down it, she'd been blown into it and slid down. We rushed over to her. Thick green blood dripped down her face from a slice in her scalp. She was dazed but alive. The Collar was in her hand, and her ivory gown was scorched and blackened in spots.

"What happened?" Megan asked her.

I tore off the hem of her gown and mopped at the blood off her face. She swatted my hand away and pulled a magic ball out of nowhere, popping it in her mouth.

"I tried to remove the gem from the Collar. It didn't like it," she snipped.

The cut was healing. Megan offered her a hand, and together the two of us pulled the much larger Fae woman up from the floor. She swayed a bit and steadied, pressing her palm to the spot where the cut had been. A headache must be lingering for a moment longer than the cut.

She looked around at her lab, her frown deepening. She rushed around checking on a few items and seemed relieved. She approached a cabinet, which appeared unharmed in the explosion, opened it, and took out a magic ball that was slightly larger than the others we'd seen. She pressed us back behind her and shuffled us out the doorway. Then she tossed the ball inside and said a word. I couldn't tell what the word was, but a cloud of vapor rose and filled the room. Dana seemed unconcerned, and she didn't say what the ball was supposed to do. She still held the collar tightly in her hand.

Megan cleared her throat. "We came down to show you some information we found in a book about the collar."

But before Dana could respond, the vapor cleared, and the entire room was spotless and returned to order. Dana looked smug. She invited us in and put the book on one of her lab tables.

"That was an awesome magic ball," I said, attempting to butter her up.

"It is a basic cleaning spell," she snipped.

Megan was flipping pages to find the section she wanted to show Dana. She'd lost the page when we were blasted in the hall.

"Ok, read this." She turned the book to Dana and pointed.

Dana leaned over and began to read. I was growing excited. She'd fix the amulet, and we'd be on our way home to defeat the vamps in no time.

She was quiet for a while, and I wondered how much she had to read. Finally, she looked up at us. "I can't do this. I don't have the elements to restart the charm on the amulet."

"What element does it need?" I asked.

Dana threw a sly look at me under her lashes. "It needs a combination of three. Time, Spirit, and Fire. They need to be woven together and forced inside the gem to reactivate the core inside."

I felt like I was being manipulated, but I did know that Dana didn't have time magic. "OK, can I lend you the one you need?" I didn't know what the game was, but she'd given me that sly look when she'd mentioned she didn't have the elements.

"No, you cannot lend the skill to me. You'll have to do it yourself."

"Me? I don't know how to enchant items!" I protested.

Megan huffed, annoyed. "Yes, you do; you do it all the time."

I waved her away. "With minor things, not something this big!" I could feel the panic like a lead ball in my chest. It was pulling me down.

"Don't be ridiculous. If Dana thinks you can do it, you can," Megan kept pushing. "You've enchanted my necklace with the ability to mind talk, protect me from elemental magic, and to read in different languages." She shrugged. "I'm with Dana. You can do it."

"Yes, with this as a guide, it won't be an issue. It's a strength and the right kind of magic, you aren't making the enchantment, only renewing it. It has faded over time," Dana added.

I put my hands up and took a step back. The onslaught was overwhelming especially with my low confidence in my magical knowledge. "Megan, what does the book say the amulet does? Is it even usable for what we want?"

She hadn't had a chance to tell me what was in the book. The explosion had scattered us, and she hadn't had a chance to show me yet.

"Yeah, it can hold power that the wearer can draw on. That wasn't its primary purpose, but it will allow us to use it that way."

"What was its original purpose?" I couldn't imagine what Merlin could offer to a Fae queen she didn't already have, so it must have been a wondrous thing.

Megan looked at Dana and cocked her hip to the side. This was a pose she took when she was unsure. "It looks like the collar was designed to enslave the wearer. If a person places the collar on another, they will obey their commands without question."

Chapter Fourteen

I looked at the collar in horror. Who'd want to do such a thing? Why? What *monster* would make it?

Good grief. I could have been enslaved. My hand flew up to my bare throat. If I hadn't put the collar on myself, I could have been the one obeying the dragons. The hair rose on the back of my neck, and I shivered.

While Megan and I spoke, Dana had continued her examination of the collar, checking whatever she saw against the book. "The slavery magic has been disabled," she stated calmly.

"If I do whatever I need to do to reactivate the thing, will it reactivate the slavery feature?"

Dana shrugged. "You might, but it isn't certain."

Maybe Merlin wasn't as big of a dick as I was imagining.

"The gem itself is a natural device for storing power. That is the intent of the gem. The collar itself is where the slavery function was added. If you avoid that area when you restart the gem, it should stay only as a power device," Dana added.

I nodded but felt sick. I didn't want an object that could enslave someone else, or worse, be turned against me and my loved ones. I'd rather leave it here in Faerie or take it straight back to the dragons. But there was the rub. I'd promised them I'd get it working before I returned it, and since I didn't want an additional problem with the dragons, I had to do it. Did the dragons know about the slavery thing? It had been turned off after all.

"OK, how do I do it?" I asked with a sigh.

Dana picked up the Collar, the huge red gem twinkling in the light. She pointed to a spot on it. "Aim your three woven elements through here, and command it to fill with the power of Faerie."

"That's it?"

She shrugged. "The complicated magic went into creating it, not turning it on or off."

I looked at the collar. It still had an aura of magic about it.

"Just remember to weave the threads together."

I groaned. I didn't know what she was talking about. "I've never done that before."

She huffed, the sound almost nearing a horse's knicker. "Watch. I'll weave water, fire, and air."

I couldn't generally see magic, but Dana did something, and as I watched, her magic lit up in three different colors. A stream of blue, orange, and cloudy white swirled from her fingers. She deftly took the strands and braided them, just like I did to my hair on occasion. When she did it, it didn't look hard.

"You try. Command it to be visible."

I pulled up my magic, until it was accessible, and commanded it to be visible. I pointed my hands at a wall, so I didn't injure anyone or destroy more of Dana's lab. She said I'd need time, spirit and fire. I pulled up my sense of time, and a purplish thread headed to the wall, next, spirit, which was clear but sparkly, and then fire, an orange stream of pure heat. They were in straight lines. The wall I aimed at was warping.

"Braid them," Dana commanded.

Since I wasn't sure how, I used my hands and wove the threads together. Once all three were braided, they grew stronger and blasted a hole through the wall even though it was several feet thick. I let the magic fall.

"That's what you need to do to the gem."

"You're sure I won't just blow us up?" I asked.

She shrugged, nonchalantly. "It's possible."

Great. My heart raced and I felt lightheaded.

"I'll wait in the hall," Megan said with a wink.

I threw her a dirty look.

Dana positioned the collar on a table, with the sturdy outer wall behind it—just in case. Now that I had a sense of how the magic felt braided, I called it up in that shape almost immediately. I aimed at the spot Dana had told me and shot the magic at the collar. The gem glowed. First, it started off softly pink, then the glow grew until it became blinding. Finally, a last bright pulse of light and I could feel that the gem was full. I stopped.

"I think that was it," I said and dropped my hands, my brow creased. Sweat dripped down my face. I brushed it away.

Dana examined the Collar. Her face as impassive as ever.

I slumped. If it hadn't worked, the dragons were gonna be disappointed, fatally so for me.

Dana turned it over a few times and stared at it. I assumed "seeing" with her gift. She nodded, and surprise of all surprises, she said, "Well done."

I nearly fainted. The most praise I'd ever received from her had been "adequate." My heart swelled with pride. It must have been good for her to compliment me. My mouth was hanging open in shock.

Megan bounced back in. Her face smug. "I knew you could do it!"

I couldn't help the smile that took over my face. "Thanks for the faith, but it wasn't a sure thing."

She blew me off with a wave of her hand. "Dana, did the slave thing reactivate?"

She was quiet. "I do not know." She frowned at the collar.

I felt a wave of uncertainty. What if I'd turned that nasty feature back on? Would I trust the collar enough to use it? Could I turn it off?

"We should test it," Megan added.

"How?" I asked.

She crossed her arms. "You put it on me and see if you can order me around. Simple."

A shiver of fear traveled down my spine. "I don't know. I don't want to enslave anyone, and I don't want to use it if it still has that feature."

"That's why we need to test it here," she said firmly. "Where it's safe."

I could see her point. What would I do if it still worked that way? Could I give it up, worse, give it back knowing it could be used to make a slave?

"Ok, let's try it out." I looked at Megan sharply. "Are you sure?"

"Yeah, I trust you. If it still works that way, you'll

remove it from me quickly, right?" Her confidence in me was scary.

"Yes, I will."

"Do it." She held out her arms.

I rolled my eyes. "I'm not putting it on your wrist."

She snorted but dropped her arms and stretched her neck.

I picked up the collar and willed it to fit over Megan's head, and it grew. I placed it over her head and settled it along her collar bones, where it shrank to fit.

"OK, it's on. What do you feel?"

"I don't feel anything." She stood stiffly.

"I'm going to give you a command, try to resist me."

She nodded. "I'm ready." She gave me a thumbs up.

I looked around. "Pick up that glass." I pointed to an empty water glass sitting on Dana's desk.

Megan looked at me, the grin still on her face. Then she frowned, and she walked slowly over to the desk and picked up the glass. She turned to me, horror written on her pale face.

She still held the glass, but her other hand reached up to grasp the collar. A visible electric spark rose from the collar and zapped her fingers. She yelped and dropped her hand. I rushed forward, commanded the collar to grow, and took it off her neck. She shivered.

"I'm so sorry," I said.

Megan rubbed her throat. "That was awful."

I searched her face to make sure she was really alright. "What did it feel like?" I asked, still feeling terrible that it had worked.

"It felt like I had no control over my body. I tried to fight it, but it sent terrible pain through my body, which only let up when I did what you commanded me to do."

I dropped the collar on the table. "I don't want it."

Chapter Fifteen

We all stared at the collar.

Megan broke the silence. "No, we need it. As long as you put it on yourself, there isn't a slave option. It'll be fine."

I looked at her. "That thing is evil."

She shook her head. "No, whoever uses it to enslave another is evil. The collar? It's just a tool. One that must be used by a *moral* person."

My heart felt full. She thought I was a good person. I mean I tried to be, but I could be tempted. What if I caught Bella or Vic? Would I enslave them to get them to stop? Would I be tempted? Was this my one ring? Would I become Sauron?

"Before you freak out, try to remove the slave feature. It was disabled before. Sure, it might have been turned off or ran out of power, but we won't know until you try. Right?"

Megan was right, before I had the full meltdown and marched the collar to Mount Doom, I should try to fix the problem. I nodded. "OK, right. I should try."

Dana put out a hand. She picked up the collar and rotated it. "Try here." she pointed to a spot to the right of the gem. "This seems to be the access point for the collar itself."

"Do I send braided magic at it? The same as before?" I asked nervously.

Dana picked up the book and scanned it. She shrugged. "We'll try that first."

Her answer was not reassuring.

"Be precise."

I stared at her. "If I'm not?"

She shrugged but lifted her hands in fists, then threw open her hands suddenly, pantomiming an explosion.

"Oh." I swallowed hard and wiped my hands down my dress, they'd started to sweat.

I took a deep breath. "Maybe you should both go back in the hall."

Megan did, but Dana just backed away a few steps.

I took a deep breath and imagined the braided strands in my mind. I gathered the magic and aimed carefully at the spot Dana had indicated. I sent a strand of will with the braided magic and let it fly. A bright flash followed, but no boom. I breathed a sigh of relief that we were all still here.

We gathered around and stared at the collar.

"Did it work?" Megan asked.

"We'll have to test it again," I replied nervously.

Megan took a step back, then stepped forward and grabbed the collar. She thrust it in my hands. "One more time." Her jaw was set, and she stood with her feet shoulder width apart and firmly planted.

I nodded and put it over her head. It shrunk.

"Pick up the glass." I repeated the initial command.

This time, Megan didn't hesitate, she went immediately and picked up the glass, and turned with panic in her eyes. "Get it off!"

I stumbled over to her, trying to move quickly, and took it off her. I let it fall to the table from my hand with a metallic clatter.

"It's not worth it," I whispered.

The room was quiet for a long time as we all stared at the collar, lost in our thoughts.

Finally, Megan broke the silence. "Look, Brigid, this can make it so we can win the war with the vamps. You can go to them now. You and Mr. Mittens. You'll be able to take the magic from Faerie with you."

I reached out a hand. It shook. I snatched it back. "No one should possess that thing. It should be destroyed."

"When we are done, we'll return it to the dragons. They've kept it from everyone else. It'll be OK."

"You'll stop me if I'm tempted?" I asked, my voice small.

"I'll stop you. But I know you'd never do it, or I wouldn't let you take it."

That was enough. My hand still shook, but I grabbed the collar and put it over my head. It shrunk to fit. If I did this, I couldn't take it off. It was too dangerous to leave lying around. It shrunk and fell heavily on my collarbones. I sighed.

Dana watched, her horsey face expressionless. "It will hold magic, but it is finite, you'll need to go back to your source and refill it often."

"How do I share the power with Mr. Mittens?" I asked.

"You should be able to *will* the collar to share the power with him. He doesn't need much, just enough to transform."

That's what he'd been telling me, but he was so reluctant to leave my land, I still wondered if there was more to it. I shrugged. "I appreciate your assistance," I told her, doing the Fae thank you by not thanking you *thing*.

She bowed her head slightly. She also handed me a bag of magic balls. "New fireballs. They explode, and the flame is unquenchable with water." She handed me another smaller bag. "Extra healing balls." She went to the bakery box and picked up another treat.

I bowed my head at her, and Megan and I headed back to the den to collect Mr. Mittens and walk home.

It was quiet at the house, since we didn't have guests. With the beginning of one problem solved—the how of being able to travel off the land and have access to power—the next step was finding the vampires, and then figuring something out to help Brightfeather. Currently, the only thing I could think of was to tell her royal in-laws about the chicks, but she didn't want to do that and I'd promised I wouldn't. If it wasn't one thing, it was another. The collar was fixed, so as long as I got it back to the dragons before my time ran out, I was good with them. Two problems checked off a large and dangerous list.

As if my list wasn't long enough, I also had an event to plan for the gargoyle's next week. At least I had a bored staff. I needed to delegate that task. So, I called Madison and put her on it. She sounded relieved. She'd been bored and was putting off looking for a new job, hoping I'd reopen soon. She was filling in at the family business as their receptionist in the meantime.

With that task off my hands, I could concentrate on the important ones. The vampires. I searched through my desk to find the letter. It was time to call Vic and set up the meeting I didn't want.

I found the number he'd left and dialed. Bella's smug voice answered.

I tensed.

"Hello," she said.

"Bella, this is Brigid." There was silence on the other end. "May I speak with Vic?"

Bella laughed, deep and throaty. "You are responding to the letter?"

"Yes," I said tersely.

"You are to leave a date and time with me. He'll meet you at the Blue Heron."

Just like the slimy vamps. He'd told me I had a choice of location, and he'd already changed it. I felt the fury burning in my bosom. I took a deep breath. At least it was public, and I knew how it was set up. It was a decent location.

I gritted my teeth. "Fine. Friday, one in the afternoon."

"Ciao." She hung up on me.

Well, it wasn't like we had pleasantries to exchange. I tucked the phone in my pocket.

Damn. I had to meet the Vendetta head in two days. Was I ready? No, but I was better prepared, and this time I could take my cat—at least to the restaurant. I doubted they allowed pets inside. I laughed. If they knew that the cat thought I was his pet, would they change the rules and throw *me* out?

Mr. Mittens was hunting meat for Brightfeather, so I'd tell him later. He'd be pissed, but we had to know where the vamps were. Somehow, I needed to get that information out of Vic.

The doorbell rang. I looked up from my desk. That was odd. I hadn't ordered anything other than the bed, and the inn was closed. There was a sign out on the highway and on the door. I frowned and stood. I went to the door and opened it. A couple stood there. A man, maybe late twenties, and a *very* pregnant woman.

"May I help you?" I asked, confused.

"I know you are closed, but everyone else in town is full. Is there any way we could beg a room?"

My face must have looked shocked, because that's how I felt.

He added hurriedly, "We'd go to the next town, but we've been driving all day, and my wife needs a break. I'm not usually like this, but we are desperate."

Well, hell. My heart went out to them. The woman looked horribly uncomfortable, but they appeared human, and it was dangerous for them to be here. On the other hand, I wouldn't see Vic for two days, and we were under an uneasy truce. My rooms were clean and ready, and Chef Jack was still employed.

Weird things happened here, though. I'd have to warn everyone to not show magic.

Megan came up behind me.

"What's going on?" She was eating an apple and took another crunchy bite right in my ear.

"These people need a room for the night."

"Aren't we closed?"

"Yes, for remodeling, but the other rooms are fine." I added the remodeling so there was a reason to be closed. It's what we'd added to the website. In truth, we'd had to repair windows and a room from a previous guest. The vampire bats had blown out the windows. The kitsune family we'd hosted last had flooded the bathroom and bedroom. They didn't tell anyone, and it'd sat the whole week they were there. It had warped the flooring, and we had to pull the entire floor up and replace it. Luckily, Luke could manage the floors in his off hours, and it was now fixed.

I looked at Megan, but I'd already made up my mind. I couldn't turn that poor woman away without a bed. She needed it. "Yes, come in, we have a room."

Megan went to the front desk and started the paperwork for the couple. Damn, I sure hoped nothing happened while they were here.

Chapter Sixteen

After Megan checked them in, and I showed them the dining facilities and the elevator, they went up to their room.

I'd put them in the room that the witch had stayed in before—the room next to Megan's on the second floor. Hopefully, Megan would pick up on anything hinky in case they weren't on the up and up.

I put out a text to everyone that we had humans on the premises and to watch their supernaturalness.

Mr. Mittens returned right after they'd gone up the elevator. The wife looked miserable and exhausted, so they were probably legit and just desperate. Since they'd only be here for the night, I wasn't that concerned.

Hmpf, was all Mr. Mittens said about it. He followed me into the bedroom and "helped" me make the bed. Which is saying he was in the way and made the process take ten minutes longer than it should have. However, it made me laugh to watch his antics. When I was done with the new bedding on the new bed, he directed me where to place his fluffy bed on top. At least, this time, he took Gabe into consideration, and had me place his bed on my side, rather than smack in the middle.

My day had been long, so while I waited for Gabe to get home from work, I soaked in my tub. Mr. Mittens sat on my vanity, while he told me about his visit with the griffins.

I crawled out and dressed in time to meet Gabe in the dining room for supper. The new couple had chosen room service, so we had the dining room to ourselves. Megan and Mr. Mittens opted to eat in the kitchen, probably to give us time alone. We had too few moments to ourselves, and we never knew when an attack would come or a problem would arise. So, we treated the moment like it was our last and made it a point to enjoy it and ignore all problems.

It was nice, even if it was over too quickly. I told Gabe all that had occurred in Faerie, and the true nature of the collar. He looked at it suspiciously.

"You're sure no one can control you with the collar now?" he asked.

"Yes, it only works that way if another person places it on you." I shuddered remembering Megan's face.

"I agree that you can't take it off until you return it," he said. "If the vamps got a hold of it…"

"I know. I don't want that either. It's irritating my skin though. I'll have to start wearing turtle necks or something."

"I'm sure you'll look great in a turtleneck," he said with a grin, picking up my distaste.

"No one looks good in a turtleneck," I grumbled.

"You can wrap this around it," he said and handed me a wrapped present. I gave him a little smile.

"What's the occasion?" I asked.

He shrugged. "I love you. We're engaged. Call it a pre-wedding gift. It's nothing big, just something that made me think of your eyes."

I kissed him and opened it. Inside was a lovely blue silk scarf. It reminded me of the skies of Faerie, but I had to agree that it matched my eyes. I quickly wrapped it around my neck, covering the collar.

"Perfect," he said and stared deeply in my eyes. "It's the exact shade."

"Thanks, I love it." I did. Plus, it was a perfect way to conceal the collar, although I needed to dig out my scarves to try to alleviate the chafing against my skin. It was high summer, but it was cool enough when it rained that I could get away with it. I had some high-necked jumpers and stuff that would work for summer and help the raw skin of my throat.

Now was a good time to tell him my other news. "I'm meeting Vic Constantine on Friday."

"No." His face was stern, his eyes unwavering.

I rolled my eyes. I knew this wasn't going to go down well.

"He wants you dead. I can't let you go. You'll be unprotected," he explained.

"Mr. Mittens will be able to come. That was the purpose of this." I pointed to the collar.

He leaned back in his chair and folded his arms. Not a good sign.

"I don't want you to go." The trump card.

I sighed. "I know. I understand why and get that you are worried. But we have to find out where to find them so we can use the collar and end this forever."

He hesitated, but I saw his resolve falter. "I want to be there."

My heart grew in my chest, filling me with warmth.

"That's fine. I doubt Mr. Mittens will be allowed in. He'll need someone to wait with him outside."

"You could make him invisible."

I blinked. I was so stupid sometimes. It was a good thing I surrounded myself with smart people. Yes. Yes, I could. Sometimes I forgot the scope of my powers. "That's a great idea."

"I can wait outside and keep Bella distracted," he said confidently.

Now it was my turn to be worried. "I don't think you should get near Bella. She's still upset you took away her immortality."

"She got it back."

"Yeah, minus all her years of building her strength. Trust me, she wants you dead."

He nodded. "Well, next time I won't stop at healing her. So, she'd better be worried about me."

My fiancé had a unique set of skills. He was a healer—a magical human who could heal wounds, fill the lifeforce well…or empty it. For vamps, that meant he could reverse their vampirism and return them to humans. Once human, he could simply take their lifeforce away. It wasn't something he would ever consider doing to an innocent and struggled to do to anyone. However, since we'd learned the true nature of a few witches and the vamps, he'd decided that true evil existed, and it had helped when he'd had to protect himself and save us.

"I know, love, but she is old, she has no scruples, and she is dangerous. Just be careful."

He smiled. "I'll be careful if you are."

"I'll have my protector. You'll be without one."

"I could take Sorcha."

I thought about it. It wasn't a bad idea, although I

wouldn't put it past the vamps to attack the house once I was gone. *We could do that, or I could always make sure everyone was in the house and place Dana's protective ward around it.*

"That might work."

"Then let's do it."

I nodded. Yeah, I needed to be smarter about this than I'd been in the past. It was time to think offensively, rather than responding defensively.

"OK, I'll talk to Sorcha tomorrow, and we'll come up with a plan."

Chapter Seventeen

The guests didn't leave. Chris and Josie Metcalf decided to have a baby in my inn instead. In their defense, I don't really think they planned it.

Josie wasn't just "not feeling well," she was in labor. She also lucked out that my fiancé was home. Shortly after our talk, as we retired for the night, Chris came tearing down the stairs in a panic. He obviously wasn't thinking straight, because most people would just call an ambulance.

"My wife is in labor," he yelled when he spotted us walking to our bedroom.

Gabe looked at me and immediately turned to the anxious father-to-be. "I'm a doctor."

The man sat down heavily on the steps. "Thank God."

"How far apart are the contractions?" Gabe asked.

The man looked up without any comprehension on his face. Gabe placed his hand on the man's shoulder. "Come on, let's go see her."

The man nodded, stood, and walked more sedately up the stairs. He was in shock.

Gabe kept a very complete medical bag. I grabbed it from the closet and followed. When Chris let us in the room, his wife Josie was pacing the floor. Her hair was in a ponytail, she was soaked with sweat, but she'd changed into a thin sleeveless nightgown. She looked up at us briefly, and then stopped, grabbed onto a chair, and panted through a contraction. Gabe whipped out his phone and timed it.

"Almost a minute."

She took a few seconds before she stood back up. Gabe continued to time.

"Hi, Josie, I'm Gabriel Ambrose. I'm a doctor, a family practitioner."

She nodded.

"I'm going to see how long between contractions, and we'll decide if we have time to get to the hospital."

She nodded again, held up a finger, and leaned into another contraction. Gabe checked his phone.

He gave me a look.

Right, it was too late.

"I'm going to have you lie down so I can examine you, Josie," Gabe said. "I think we might be delivering this baby here."

I hurriedly stripped the bed to the sheets and threw down clean towels. Josie continued to pace.

"What do you need?" I asked Gabe.

"Stay here, I need to wash and find gloves and supplies."

He hurried to the bathroom, while I attempted to keep both soon-to-be parents calm.

He came back out, wearing a paper gown and gloves.

Josie lay on the prepared bed, and Gabe performed a quick exam.

"She's fully dilated," he said to the husband. "I want

you to call the ambulance; they'll need to take her and the baby in, but she's having the child here."

Chris nodded, but he swayed. I grabbed him by the arm and guided him to the chair that Josie had been using.

"It's three weeks early," he mumbled.

"That's why we're calling that ambulance," Gabe reassured him.

He nodded at me, and I took out my phone. Chris wasn't in a head space for this. I dialed 911.

Josie was bearing down.

"This is going fast," Gabe warned me.

There wasn't anything I could do but try to keep Chris calm. Josie seemed to be doing well. Of course, she was in very good hands. Here, Gabe could use his magic on mother and baby to keep them healthy as they went through their ordeal.

"One more push, and the shoulders are through," Gabe said encouragingly.

Chris fainted. By the time I had his feet up and him covered with a blanket, the baby was screaming. I looked over to see Gabe wrap it in a blanket, the cord already cut. He handed the child to the new mama while waiting for the delivery of the afterbirth. The baby was small, but perfect. The dad asked his wife how she was from the floor, and she replied that she was happy. Tears ran down her face as she gazed on the tiny new person in her arms. It was magical.

I looked on the scene with love for Gabe and longing for the children I'd never have. Our eyes met.

His eyes were overly bright, I could tell he was also touched. I guess mine were, too, because I felt the tears roll down my face. If he did go through with the wedding, this was something I couldn't give him. Even with my extended lifetime, which may have made it possible for me to have a child long past childing bearing age on earth, the equipment was gone. I looked away from Gabe. I didn't want him to see my pain.

We'd need to talk about this later. I finally had the new dad back up in the chair. His color was better, and we needed to care for mom, so I took the babe and placed it in his arms. He looked at his daughter with wonder. Gabe finished up with mom just in time for the sirens of the ambulance to come into hearing. I ran down to let the EMTs in. This time, they were normal humans—no weird vamps faking it.

Before we knew it, the new family was safely on their way to the hospital, and we were left cleaning up.

Gabe stuffed his used gear into a garbage bag as I stripped the bed. "I can't give you children." I blurted out, all the emotion from the birth choking my voice. He needed to know, and I couldn't hold it back. He deserved more than I could give him.

He looked at me. "I know, Brigid."

"If you marry me, you'll lose your chance," I said.

He laughed.

I stood up straight and looked at him, hands on my hips—tears gone. A flicker of anger filled me. "Why are you laughing?"

"Brigid, if we want children, we can always adopt or get a surrogate. But look around. We have griffin babies, we have a very strange cat, we have a teen dragon. I think we're blessed. We have so much more than I could have dreamed. I'm happy with all you're giving me by offering to share your crazy life."

I jumped into his arms and kissed him until he forgot his name. I might have forgotten mine as well.

Chapter Eighteen

Chris, the baby's father, returned in the morning. Luckily, he just picked up their things and thanked us for our help. The hotel next to the hospital had a vacancy, and it made more sense than driving out of town. The baby was doing OK, but since it was a little early, they were keeping it in NICU for a few days. He thanked us again and left.

For being closed, we'd still managed to have a crazy guest experience. I felt relieved that they'd left. I was still waiting for the ax to fall with either the vamps or the griffins. I hadn't checked on Brightfeather for a few days, so I decided that I would. Gabe went to work early; he wanted to be back for the vamp showdown at the Blue Heron.

Megan had gone to town to do something with Luke. I hadn't been paying close attention, but it was something to do with a job he had. Mr. Mittens went with me.

We realm walked to Brightfeather's nest. It seemed like every time I went, the chicks had noticeably grown. We walked in to see that the nest was getting crowded. The three chicks were starting to shed their fluff and looked disheveled with their adult feathers poking through here and there. Little Umber was the largest. He was going to be a stout griffin when he grew up. He'd probably be bigger than his father. Brightstorm was maturing nicely, but little Brigid seemed a lot smaller than her brothers. Maybe it was because she was an owl griffin rather than an eagle like them, maybe because she was female, or maybe it was because she was underdeveloped because of her difficult hatching. I didn't know, but she was my favorite.

She had the most personality. Her mother had always been steady and dependable, but little Brigid was full of adventure. She was the one that had to be constantly brought back from the edge of the nest, to be stopped from going outside. They weren't big enough yet to venture out alone. Each was about half the size of the unicorn foal or a large pony foal. They were growing quickly, though, and would be ready to go outside the nest and start strengthening their wings soon enough.

"Hello, Brightfeather," I said.

She stood and shook out her feathers. She still looked rough, locked in a pattern of single parenthood and grief from the loss of her mate. Stress was probably part of the equation as well.

She nodded to me.

"We can watch them if you want a break," I offered.

She thought for a moment and thanked us. *It would be nice to stretch my wings and hunt. Maybe I can also have a quick bath in the waterfall.*

She sure looked like she needed one.

"I'm sorry I haven't been around as much as I promised," I said to her.

Her eyes were soft. *I'm grateful for all of you, and what you, Megan, and Mr. Mittens do for us. Do not worry, Lady Brigid.*

I shook my head. She knew I hated the "lady" thing. I just smiled, though. She left, and the chicks decided it would be fun to wrestle with their cat uncle. At least there was room with Brightfeather gone. It became a melee of fur and feathers, and soon enough they collapsed into a pile of exhausted and sound asleep griffinettes. My cat was a great babysitter. I looked at him fondly as he lay curled around the chicks, purring a loud raspy purr.

I adored them as well. I couldn't bear to have them leave and go back with the griffins. I had to come up with something to keep them and Brightfeather here. I sighed, and Mr. Mittens looked at me, his periwinkle eyes large and knowing.

If we have to take them to Faerie we will, he said.

"That's the last resort. If we do that, we'll have to leave here forever," I argued.

Would that be so terrible?

I imagine that for a being that was more or less exiled from his own realm, that was a loaded question. For me, obviously I'd prefer to live on earth. It was my home, but I had links to Faerie. If I moved there permanently, it would force Gabe and Megan to as well. I couldn't ask that of them. Megan had Luke here and a new life. Gabe had his practice, which I didn't see him wanting to give up. I had the house and the land that I adored, but I loved my friends here as well.

It was a dilemma I just couldn't solve and didn't want to think about.

Mr. Mittens must have read me, or my thoughts leaked out. *Let's deal with the vampires, and we'll figure out the griffins.*

I nodded again. Yes, yes, we would. I didn't know how, but we had to. I needed to stay focused on the vamps right now. Once they were gone, we'd have some breathing room.

Brightfeather came back, walking quietly in. She looked much better—clean and refreshed.

Thank you so much for getting them to sleep, she said. *They've been wearing me ragged lately.*

"That was all Mr. Mittens," I replied.

We talked quietly a few minutes more, then left, walking back to the house in an instant. I had a couple of hours left before my meeting, and I wanted to be physically and mentally prepared. I packed a variety of Dana's magic balls in my pocket, filled the Golden Collar of Merlin with Fae magic, and loaded my engagement ring with a few more spells. I'd done it for Megan, though this was the first time I'd thought of doing something similar for myself. It was a failing I needed to correct.

Once done, I dressed carefully. Gabe walked in as I was choosing my outfit and kissed me on the neck. He was going to keep watch outside for Bella or any other vamp spying or looking to make trouble and stay as back up with Sorcha. Mr. Mittens would go with us, and I'd cast shadow magic on him so he could enter the restaurant as further protection for me. Now that I was dressed and ready, reality struck, and my knees wobbled. I sat on the bed and tried to calm my racing heart and shaking limbs.

Gabe put his arm around me, attempting to comfort me. "Mr. Mittens and I have your back. You'll be safe," he crooned in my ear.

What he didn't realize was I wasn't afraid for me. If they killed me, everyone I loved was in danger. That's what terrified me. I reached up and put my hand on his face. Then I kissed him.

Yes, this was why I fought the vamps. They wouldn't push me off my land; they wouldn't hurt my friends. I chanted that in my mind, and somewhere I found my courage again.

"I'm ready," I said to Gabe. He pulled me up, and together with Mr. Mittens, we headed to the car where Sorcha waited.

Chapter Nineteen

It was a typical Northern Oregon Coast summer day—overcast, hovering at about sixty degrees Fahrenheit, and drizzly. I was hoping for sunlight to limit the vamps. When we pulled up to the barn-like structure of the restaurant, I scanned for Bella or any other noticeable vampire. Since it was summer, there were a lot of tourists. Several families were enjoying the little petting zoo, some were examining the old logging equipment lying around, and people walked back and forth from the parking lot.

"Do you see her?" I asked my companions.

"No," Gabe said, scanning the area.

Sorcha gave a negative sounding grunt.

Mr. Mittens flicked his ears around and sniffed, but he also didn't spot anyone.

"I'll go look at the petting zoo and look around while you're inside," Gabe said. I nodded, but my stress levels were sky high.

"I'll search around the building," Sorcha added. She

wasn't as able to fit in, being a seven-foot-tall woman, so I offered her concealing magic, and she agreed.

I used my shadow magic to conceal Sorcha and Mr. Mittens. I couldn't see him anymore, so I reminded him to stay close. I continued scanning the area as I walked around the building to the door.

It was crowded inside. "Be careful, Mr. Mittens," I said silently. I didn't want him getting stepped on just because no one could see him.

Hmpf. I am a cat, was his snooty response.

I rolled my eyes, but his steady presence and expected response did relieve my anxiety by a tiny bit. My shoulders dropped an inch.

I walked around to the lunch counter and immediately spotted Vic. He was seated at the same table I'd met him at before. The difference was he was with someone. A female. Her back was to me. I squinted at them. It wasn't Bella, unless she'd changed her hair. I cautiously skirted the table so that I could see who it was and judge the danger I was in.

As I circled around, I recognized the woman. Amber Bergman, aka June North, my fake cousin and fake psychic. She was really a witch, the sister of my dead nemesis Sofia, and apparently a vampire as well.

I froze, and as I did, Vic noticed me. He stood and pulled out a chair for me. For a slimy, blood sucking bastard, he had manners. I settled in, and after he pushed me back to the table, I felt Mr. Mittens lean against my legs. It was comforting.

Vic introduced me, "Brigid, this is my wife, Amber. Amber, Brigid."

"We've met," I said dryly.

He smiled. "Not officially."

"Yeah, last time she was spying and trying to steal my magic." I didn't feel like playing whatever game this was.

Last time I'd seen Amber, she had been drained nearly to death from overusing her witch's well. Her life force was almost gone. She had aged to an ancient woman and looked frail and white-haired.

She'd been healed by being changed into a vamp. She now appeared to be a young woman in her prime. Her hair was long and honey blonde, nearly the same shade as her sister's had been. The family resemblance was visible now. I realized she'd done something to her appearance before, or I would have noticed. For one, her hair had been brown.

"So, why am I here?" I asked, trying to cut through the bullshit.

Vic chuckled, a dark throaty sound. He sipped from a glass of wine. I finally noticed that the table had three bottles of wine and a selection of cheeses on a board.

"Please, before we talk business, refresh yourself." He waved a hand over the table.

I wasn't hungry, not in the least. My stomach was in knots. However, I took a few slices of cheese and poured some wine. I picked up a piece of cheese and pretended to nibble on it. Then I palmed it and slipped it under the table. Mr. Mittens' whiskers tickled as he plucked it from my fingers. I couldn't help a small smile from forming.

I took a sip of the wine. It was fruity, a perfect complement to the cheese I couldn't eat. I set it back down. I wasn't in the mood, and I'd completed the pleasantries. "What is this about? You wanted to parley, what do you have to offer?"

He glanced at his wife. "I met my Amber when she was seventeen. An utterly enchanting creature." He reached over and stroked a finger down her cheek. She smiled and leaned into his touch.

I shuddered.

"She was young, so I wooed her for a few years until she was fully grown and a woman by your modern standards."

He sipped his wine, and Amber continued to gaze lovingly on him. I wondered if she'd been compelled or was really that stupid.

"The coven agreed to the marriage. Mainly so they could benefit financially from the arrangement. I brought in businesses, and my sister-in-law ran them. It was a small part of my empire, but it made the coven happy."

Amber reached over and patted his hand.

I almost gagged.

"Then came my sister-in-law's obsession with you, dear Brigid. Once she realized you didn't take after your witch forebears, but were Fae, she wouldn't stop with her desire to take that infinite well of power from you. In fact, she talked about nothing else, from when she was"—he looked at his wife—"a teen?"

She nodded.

"Of course, I knew nothing of this until later. It all came to a head a few years after you moved away. The new owners of the house abandoned it quite early, although they kept up payments for a few years. No matter how many forays we took to search the house for the missing magic and the books and journals written by your ancestors on how to take it, we didn't find anything. It seems they won't reveal themselves until a member of the family is near. So clever, your ancestors." He shook his head and tsked. "Then you came back, and well, you know the rest of the story."

I did. His creepy sister-in-law befriended me and tried to kill me more than once.

"Why are you telling me this?" I was growing angry. It was like he brought me here to mock me. Every time we met; it was surreal. Like he was two different people. A killer and this old-world gentleman who was trying to have a civilized conversation over a meal. I almost couldn't deal with it.

He leaned in, his dark eyes sparkling with mirth. "Because I know something that you would find deeply important."

I wrinkled my brow. What was he talking about, what was the game? If I asked what he was talking about, he'd enjoy withholding it from me. The curiosity burned a hole in my stomach, but I couldn't let him know I cared.

I shrugged.

Chapter Twenty

I cut another piece of cheese and set it on my plate. "So, what are the terms of the parley?"

He glanced at his wife. "I will give you this information freely, if you agree to fill my wife's well."

"That's what you had me come here for?" I looked away, trying to pull my anger in so I could think clearly. "And you think that for some piece of information you think I'll want, that I'll have my fiancé fill your wife's well so she can use her witch magic against us?"

He frowned and leaned in, serious. "I will make an oath that she will not use her witchcraft against you or yours."

He thought I'd go for that? "Hmpf." I was now copying Mr. Mittens. "But will she make such an oath on her magic?" I folded my arms.

He looked at her thoughtfully, and she nodded, tersely.
"She will."

That astonished me. I wondered why they were so desperate to get her power back. She'd fully drained it when she'd tried to steal my magic. The spell had rebounded on her, and instead of locking me away from my power, she'd done it to herself. I didn't want to return that power to her, because whatever they wanted it for had to be bad. At the same time, I wasn't sure it could be returned to her.

"What if it doesn't work?"

He gave a casual shrug. "We believe we've solved that problem, but as long as you try in good faith, I'll give you the information."

I took a deep breath. I didn't like it, and I didn't want Gabe to do it. Especially, since I had no idea if the information he was peddling was something I needed or could use. It might be something stupid or useless, and we'd have given them a huge gift, that no matter what oaths they took would somehow come back to bite us. I was as sure of that as I was that Mr. Mittens was pressed against my leg.

"To what does this information pertain?"

He smiled, and a chill ran down my spine. "I know something about your new piece of jewelry." He pointed at my throat.

The chill turned into icy fingers gripping my heart. How did he know anything about the collar? I'd only just discovered it and its properties. Did I still have spies on my land?

Mr. Mittens growled quietly. I could only tell because I could feel it rattle his body. All I had to do was feed him a tiny bit of power, and he could transform. Together, we could kill both these creatures. Consequences be damned. I gripped the edge of the table until my knuckles turned white.

"I'll pass." I stood up, and the chair slid back with an ugly scraping sound. I felt Mr. Mittens move forward to put his body between me and the vamps.

"Do this for us, and I'll add an incentive. One year of peace."

Shit. That was pretty sweet. In a year, I could take care of the griffins and have time to prepare better defenses while creating better ways to destroy the vamps. However, they'd have a year to rebuild their numbers as well. Plus, whatever they needed the witch's power for.

I shook my head and took a step to leave.

"My last offer is five years."

I hesitated. Maybe in that time they'd forget about me and the inn? No, that was more time for them.

"Not worth it." I made it five steps.

Vic used vamp speed and stopped me by stepping in front of me. He made a gesture, and Bella stepped into the dining room, her arm looped through Gabe's. Crap, where was Sorcha? Was she OK? Gabe looked stunned, his eyes unfocused. I wondered why he hadn't healed her or killed her. He needed only to touch her to do that, so she'd done something to him to stop it.

Sunlight blazed in my hands. I lifted them towards Vic, who raised his hands to block the powerful light.

He smiled. "You can put that away. It won't harm me, and although it will harm my wife, we don't want that to happen, do we?" He opened his mouth slightly, and his canines extended. "Now then, how about you have your fiancé fill my wife's well, I'll give you my information, and we'll all leave."

"What about the five years of peace?"

"Well, you should have taken my offer. Now that's off the table. But I'll have what I came for, and since I'm a generous fellow, I'll still give you the information, I'm not unreasonable." These last words had a slight lisp said through his extended teeth, and on top of the stress, it tickled my funny bone a little. I had to hold back a hysterical laugh.

I could feed magic into Mr. Mittens; I was sure he could decapitate Vic before he could do much. The vamp couldn't see him after all. But Bella would kill Gabe just as quickly. I frowned. I couldn't see a way out. It was a checkmate situation. I had to give him what he wanted. Damn it all.

"Fine, let go of him. He'll fill her well."

I caught Gabe's eyes. The second Bella let go of him, his gaze cleared, and he looked at me, confused. He looked around the room and realized what was going on.

"Gabe, Vic has asked that you fill the witch's well. Then we can leave."

"Are you sure?"

"Yes."

He didn't look very willing, and his jaw was clenched. "What happens if I don't?"

Vic gave another slow smile. His teeth had retracted. "Well, we also have your other friend."

Impossible, how could they see her? Gabe and I exchanged a look.

"Let's just get it over with," I said.

He hesitated a moment more, then moved to the table where the witch vamp remained seated, still smiling vapidly. She had to be under some kind of controlling spell or vamp charm.

He looked up at me and placed his hands on her head. The familiar warmth of his magic touched me. After a few seconds, he dropped his hands. "It's done."

Vic smiled. "Now that wasn't so bad, was it?"

Bella moved to his side, and I grabbed Gabe and drew

him back from the vamps. Mr. Mittens was spitting mad. I could feel the waves of rage pouring off of him.

Let me kill them now, he said.

"I wish I could, but we'd scare all of these families and be on the news if I let you."

Worth it, he huffed.

"You'll have your chance soon." I turned to leave.

"Don't you want your information?" Vic said, and I turned reluctantly back to him.

"What is it?"

He gave a little half smile. That wasn't good.

"The maker of the lovely neck adornment you wear is still very much alive." He waved at Bella who handed me a piece of paper. I tucked it in my pocket, not taking my eyes off the vamps.

He gestured to his wife, who stood, and the three of them left.

I let out a whoosh of air. I hadn't realized I'd been breathing shallowly, and I gasped in a full breath. I looked Gabe over. "What did she do to you?"

He lifted up his shirt, so I could see his side. It had a two-pronged burn. "She tased me. It locked me up, and I couldn't access my power."

"Where's Sorcha?"

He shrugged helplessly, so we hurried out and started looking. I felt for the magic I'd used to hide her, and once I sensed it, I released it from her. She was lying by some of the logging equipment that was part of the landscaping around the building. She groaned as we approached, then leapt to her feet, ready to fight.

"It's us, they're gone," I said.

She put her hand on her lower back. "That bitch vamp shot me with lightning," Sorcha griped.

She'd been tased, too. I wonder how Bella had found her through my shadow magic. It must have started wearing thin.

I nodded. Sometimes simple and mundane was as effective as magic. "Let's go home."

Chapter Twenty-One

Gabe had me look at the paper once we were safely ensconced in the car and on our way home. Mr. Mittens grumbled that I'd taken him off the property and not let him kill anything. I unfolded the paper and glanced at it. It was a phone number.

I crumpled it up. "It's a phone number," I groused.

"Do you think it belongs to Merlin?" Gabe asked.

"I don't know. This was all a setup, it's probably just the local weather channel." I couldn't believe they'd manipulated us into giving Amber her magic back. That was definitely bad. I was such a fool. I couldn't believe that I'd gone in thinking we'd get the upper hand. We'd been outsmarted on all fronts. I looked at the number again. Part of me wanted to throw it out the window in a fit of pique. But a tiny part really did wonder if I could call the number and Merlin the enchanter would answer. I shook my head at my foolishness. This was just another vampire game.

"We should still call," Gabe insisted.

"What if it's an elaborate trap?" I was learning. It had

taken months and me trusting the wrong people to do it, but I was getting there.

"We'll deal with it then. A call is harmless. Let's see what's on the other side of the line."

I agreed to call when we got back to the house. I was too worked up to think straight at the moment. The collar felt like it was choking me. I knew it was psychological but still. It *felt* real enough. I put my finger along the edge and tried to pull it away from my throat. It didn't give. I sighed.

Why would Vic tell us Merlin was alive? If he knew about the collar, he knew what it did and why I'd wanted it. I still didn't know where the vamps were holed up, unless it was back at the warehouse, but I sincerely doubted it. I didn't think they were somewhere I'd find quickly. We'd decimated their numbers, and he had to be hurting from those losses. I think part of his ploy was to throw us off and keep us from attacking for a while, so he could rebuild his numbers. He also needed a witch for something. Something he was willing to take an oath not to use on us.

Damn it. I'd forgotten to get the oath. I slapped my palm on my forehead.

"What's wrong?" Gabe asked.

"I'm an idiot," I said. "I let them leave without taking an oath not to use Amber's witch powers against us."

"They'd never have done that, Brigid. Don't take it too hard."

I nodded. Of course. It was all to sweeten the deal and convince me it wasn't that important, but it had been their plan all along. They'd never intended to take an oath. I'd been fooled again.

"I might have filled her well, Bridge, but she didn't have a very deep one. Whatever they have planned, is either small, or they have a plan to keep her topped off. She only has one large spell in her. Although, now she's a vamp, draining it won't kill her like it would before. She'd just be magicless."

"Well, knowing them, they have a backup plan to steal my magic," I said snippily.

"That was always the plan."

"True." That had been Sofia's goal, it was her sister's goal, and the vamps wanted me dead, so that aligned as well.

Gabe pulled into the long drive that led to the house.

"Stop the car, please," I asked quietly.

He slowed to a stop.

I climbed out of the car, faced away, and screamed at the top of my lungs until I'd expelled every scrap of air from them. I doubled over and grabbed my knees. After I refilled my lungs with air, I climbed back in the car. Mr. Mittens hopped over the divider from the back seat and curled up in my lap. It was his way of offering comfort. I stroked his cottony fur and let the peace of his love fill me.

Gabe parked. He didn't say a word about my little fit. He must have recognized that I needed to let it out. Sorcha was still sulking about being tased. I doubted anyone would be able to pull that on her again. We walked in the back kitchen door, but Sorcha peeled away and headed to the dairy. No one was in the kitchen.

Mr. Mittens jumped onto the old oak table, and Gabe settled in one of the chairs. I pulled out the paper and my phone and dialed the number. Gabe and Mr. Mittens watched me.

The phone rang three times, and a strong masculine voice answered. "Hello?"

I really didn't expect a person to answer. Maybe the weather, or some other information number. My voice caught in my throat—I didn't know what to say. If Vic wasn't pulling my chain, this was Merlin. Did he go by Merlin still? Myrddin? Bob? I had no idea.

After a very long few seconds, I finally said, "Umm, hi. My name is Brigid. Is this Merlin?"

Silence.

"How did you get this number?"

It wasn't going to do any good holding stuff back. Vic already knew of the collar, and if this was Merlin, he might be able to help us out if he wasn't in deep with the vampires.

"I have the collar. I was hoping to ask you some questions about it."

"Is this a joke?" he growled. "Who is this?"

"Not a joke. I told you my name is Brigid. I'm Fae, I heard you were too. Any chance we could meet?" I cringed at the words coming out of my mouth, but there was no easy way to say it. If this was just some random guy, he'd think I was a kook and hang up.

"No." The phone disconnected. I guess he thought I was a kook.

I looked at Gabe and Mr. Mittens. "That was a real guy. If it was really Merlin, he's a bit of a dick."

Hmpf, Mr. Mittens said.

"He's probably just in shock and doesn't like people," Gabe added, always the kind one.

We don't need him. The collar is working.

I scratched Mr. Mittens behind the ears. "You're right. I did want to meet him, but it isn't necessary."

Megan walked through the door from the house, Luke on her heels. "What's going on?"

"I just talked to Merlin on the phone," I said.

Her mouth dropped open. "The Merlin?"

"Yup."

"Damn, girl."

He was a dick to Brigid, Mr. Mittens added.

Megan laughed.

Luke looked between us, confused. "I've missed something."

"The collar thing that Brigid is wearing?" Megan started. "Well, it was made by Merlin a long time ago. We thought we'd have to find him to get it fixed, but Brigid fixed it with Dana's help. You're all caught up."

He shrugged. "So, normal stuff?"

We all laughed.

My phone rang. I looked at it, expecting a telemarketer. I put up a hand and shushed everyone. "It's him, calling me back."

They all shut up. "Hello?" I answered.

"I'll meet you." That was it. The phone went click.

I felt the pulse of magic and whirled around. A strange man appeared in my kitchen.

Chapter Twenty-Two

I might have squeaked and dropped my phone. I will deny it, though. "Merlin?" I asked stupidly.

He was average height and looked human, not high Fae, although his magic felt very familiar. He had brown hair, cut short, and looked like he was somewhere in that thirty to fifty age group—old enough you could tell he was firmly an adult male, but not so you could really place his age. His eyes were intensely green. Luke had green eyes, but they were more like moss, Merlin's were like spring grass.

He wasn't particularly handsome or plain, but interesting. He was dressed in jeans and a t-shirt that said, "In my defense, I was left unsupervised."

I stared.

"Yeah, I'm Merlin." I was expecting a British accent, but it was more a rolling lilt, like he was Welsh or Irish.

"How did you find me?" I asked, astonished. My grandfather and Dana always appeared where I was, and I'd meant to ask how they did it. Apparently, it was something

Merlin could do as well, although we'd never met, and as far as I knew, he'd never been here.

He frowned. "You aren't a very good Fae, are you?"

"I'm just learning. I only found out about this a year ago," I said a little defensively. It was more than a year, but I'd taken one of Dana's magic balls to forget my first foray into magic.

"Hmm."

He looked around, his gaze caught on Mr. Mittens. "Nice cat."

Mr. Mittens flicked his tail. I cut him off before he could say anything.

"He's a Ragdoll."

Mr. Mittens glared at me. I aimed a tight mental message to him. *We don't know if he's friend or foe, so let's keep some of our secrets.*

Hmpf. He lay down on the table and began to groom himself like any naughty cat. I put a hand on him and stroked his fur.

Merlin peered at my neck. "Yes, that is my collar. How did you get it? I gave it to the dragons."

"From the dragons," I answered. Megan gave a choked laugh and hurried to cover it with a cough.

"Hmmm." Merlin approached me and reached out a hand to touch the collar.

Gabe was on his feet and stood to intercept him.

Merlin dropped his hand. "I don't mean any harm; I only wish to examine it."

I shook my head, and Gabe stood his ground. Merlin backed away.

"So, what did you want to ask? You called me, remember?"

I remembered my manners and offered him a seat. The

table could sit eight comfortably, ten if you really liked your guests. The five of us sat.

"Can you tell us about the collar?"

He glanced at each one of us, trying to read the room, I assumed. "You must know something, because you are wearing the collar, and I can sense it's been activated."

"We know a little, but we also discovered it is a slave collar, perhaps you should start there."

Merlin stiffened. "How did you learn that?"

I shrugged, not wanting to give anything of ours away. "Why would you make a slave collar out of an object meant as a wedding gift?"

He smiled. It didn't reach his eyes. "That was the commission. The new bridegroom wanted the option to control the bride. He wanted to rule, but he didn't want to share the throne, even though it was her queendom. He was late on the payment, I wasn't comfortable with the purpose, so I sold it to the dragons."

He'd left something out of that story, I sensed, like why did he do it if he was uncomfortable? Was it a Fae thing, a geas?

"Did the dragons know it could enslave them?"

"I turned off that function. It was only a magical storage device to them."

"Why did it quit working?"

"It has to have magic to store, or it will sleep."

"Sleep?" I choked. "Is it sentient?"

"Not exactly. Let's say it has some unique properties."

I reached up and stuck my finger under the Collar again, attempting to pull it away from my neck. "Like what properties?"

He shrugged but didn't answer. Merlin's eyes had

followed my action. "If you placed it around your own neck, you have nothing to fear."

I dropped my hand.

"It seems you already know the collar's secrets, why did you need me?"

I took a deep breath. "We were wondering if you could make another."

He looked taken aback.

"I've not crafted such an item for many years, and there's not much magic on earth…" He looked around. "You have a link to Faerie." His gaze sharpened on me. "Who did you say you were?"

"I haven't, not really."

"Where are we?"

"Oregon coast."

His green-eyed gaze looked at me sharply. "You are the child of Lugh Pendragon."

I recoiled, shocked. "I am."

He stood from his chair. it rocked back and crashed to the ground. He knelt.

"My lady."

What the hell?

Chapter Twenty-Three

We looked around at each other in shock. Mr. Mittens stood up and stared down at the enchanter.

I can eat him if you wish, he said.

"Please don't, I have questions," I replied silently. Then I turned to Merlin. "What is this all about?"

I knew the Arthur myths, sort of, at least as much as anyone learned through school literature growing up. I knew his father had been Uther Pendragon. But I assumed my grandfather's title was just that, a title, not a name from a myth. How was he related to Uther? *Was* he related to Uther and Arthur?

My hands shook; I clasped them together and put them on my lap.

Megan stood up, grabbed an apple from a basket on the fruit basket, and leaned against the counter. She polished it on her pants and took a bite. "I love it here." She kept her eyes on Merlin. A grin on her face as she chewed.

"How do you know my great grandfather?"

"Great grandfather?" he repeated.

"Yes."

He nodded. "That makes sense, it has been many years."

"So?" My voice had risen in pitch. I was freaked out a bit. I wasn't even sure why, other than the strangeness of the whole thing. I was talking to Merlin, he knew my grandfather, he might even be a relative. Or I was just jumping to conclusions.

He sighed, straightened his chair and sat back down. "It is a long story."

I looked at everyone, they were also fascinated. "I think we're OK with that."

"Fine. Hasn't your grandfather ever spoken of me?"

"No." The truth was I hadn't had a chance to ask him, but he obviously had something to do with Merlin, since he had those books.

Merlin looked down and placed his hands on the table, staring at them. He was missing the pointer finger on his right hand. He moved his hands back to his lap.

"I'm not sure where to start, but since I'm sure you want to know about Arthur, I'll start there."

Megan moved around and sat on Luke's lap, and they got settled. Mr. Mittens sat back down and stared at Merlin from the table.

"I'm half Fae. I realm walk, as you know, so I spent a lot of time traveling back and forth, making my fortune, developing my magic."

"One day, in this realm, I came upon a burnt-out cottage. It contained the remains of a family. Mother, father, and two children, dead. I almost passed by, keeping an eye out for highwaymen, when I heard the cry of a babe. I thought of just moving on, briefly, but I couldn't leave it to suffer. I determined I'd go put it out of its misery, assuming it was burned or injured.

"I found the babe stuffed under the roots of a tree in a basket filled with rags to keep it warm and cushioned. I plucked it up and saw it was uninjured. One of the family had hidden it before whatever disaster befell them.

"I couldn't kill it; it was perfectly healthy. I determined I'd find it a family to care for it. So, I gathered him up."

He cleared his throat. Taking the hint, I stood and grabbed him a bottle of water; he gave me a thankful nod, took a drink, and continued.

"I looked around but found I really couldn't part with him. I'd grown quite fond of him you see, so I taught him all I knew and took him realm walking with me. I don't know how it happened, but my adopted son, Arcturus as I named him, grew to be a patriot of his home country. Even though our time there was limited to a month here, a year there, etc. As he observed his country being torn apart by various invaders, he decided that he'd do something about it.

"His first goal was to learn all he could of warfare. The Romans still occupied Britain when Arcturus was small. Although he held them in contempt, he found the Roman occupiers to be fierce and disciplined soldiers. So, his first step was to join up and learn their ways. Now remember, even though Arcturus was human, we'd realm walked and spent time in Faerie. And although the boy looked about fifteen when he joined up with the legions, several hundred years had passed since he'd been born. He'd had an extensive education and was fascinated with war and tactics. He rose quickly in the ranks, but ultimately, he wanted to make Britain free.

"We left again and went back to Faerie, and as an expert

in earth tactics, he joined with an upcoming tactician and warrior, a powerful Fae lord."

I looked up sharply, "My grandfather?"

"Yes."

"Lugh offered further experience. He trained with Arcturus, and they developed fighting skills and tactics together and became a fighting force to be reckoned with."

"Meanwhile, since Arcturus was busy following this course, I had been developing my enchanted items and figuring out how to store and mix elements and powers. At the time, right before the high king's rule, the land was divided into four courts—Summer, Winter, Autumn, and Spring. Each court ruled their own areas and peoples. I was hired by a high Fae lord to create the collar for his marriage to the Autumn Queen.

"It was a mess, there was unrest already occurring as the populace grew tired of the government structure, and who ran what, and who could travel between each realm—you know the whole bureaucracy of government." He waved a hand to dismiss it.

"The new consort—who wasn't royal, wasn't anything really besides wealthy—had great ambitions. He ordered me to put the slave function in the collar and disguise it as a vessel to hold immense amounts of magic.

I interrupted him. "Why did you do it?"

Merlin stared at me, then decided he had nothing to lose. "I owed him a favor. You know the Fae and their rules. I couldn't find a way out of the request."

I did know. He could have done something as small as thank him or had received a favor and found himself in debt.

"You know the rest. He didn't pay me on time, and I

used that as an excuse to get out of the geas. I took the collar and fled back to earth."

"Arcturus wasn't ready to put his plan into action. He needed experience, and the Collar incident would give it to him. It was the impetus for the war that led to the current reign of the High King of Faerie—although it wasn't the entire reason. Needless to say, your grandfather and Arcturus stood with the current king. After he conquered the other courts and became high king, he raised Lugh to the role of Pendragon. Lugh made Arcturus his second. Arcturus would have inherited the title if Lugh had fallen."

He sighed and looked away for a moment. "Someone on earth must have heard that tale from Arcturus himself— that's how the Pendragon stories began. Anyway, Lugh didn't fall, and after a while, Arcturus decided it was time to begin his goal of freeing England from the remnants of Rome and the new invaders from the north countries."

"What about Excalibur and the Lady of the Lake and stuff?" Megan asked.

He chuckled. "Well, I had to arrange something spectacular to help Arcturus earn his way quickly into a kingdom and an army. So, I came up with the sword in the stone thing. It wasn't hard to do, and only required a few years, a realm walk, and some gossip. I placed it sometime after the war—thanks to the time deferential between earth and Faerie, years on earth had passed—yet it remained, having built its own mythology in the meantime. Once we returned, Arthur pulled the sword out, and I declared him king."

"What was the deal with the Lady of the Lake?" Megan pressed.

He shook his head. "That was real."

"Was it the same sword?"

Merlin shook his head. "Swords aren't meant to stay out in the weather, shoved in rock for years. I'd just commissioned a decent sword from a local blacksmith. It wasn't anything special; I just needed to get attention.

"However, Arthur did need something special to meet his goal and impress his armies. I commissioned a sword, and more importantly a magical sheath from the Fae. There is a brilliant enchanter in Faerie. She can make items of great magic, and she is frightfully clever about it. She can even make items that are beyond her magical scope. Before the current monarchy, she worked alone on the banks of a lake. Being part kelpie, she liked being near water, and she was given the title Lady of the Lake."

Chapter Twenty-Four

I gasped. "Dana?"

He nodded. "She crafted the sword and sheath and presented them to Arcturus. The sword could be set aflame and was made of the finest Fae steel, which is enchanted to be stronger than earth steel but contains no iron. However, because of its magical nature, it would shear through any earthly weapon. The sheath was bespelled to heal any wounds."

We nodded. I think we'd all heard that before in the tales of Arthur. My mind was still reeling, thinking about Dana as the Lady of the Lake. I guess all those medieval paintings of her as a beautiful woman were propaganda. Her terrifying visage wouldn't make as good of a story. However, she was powerful and talented.

"The rest, although glorified and fanciful, was more or less true, Arcturus set out to find heroes for his new kingdom and set up armies to achieve his goal. After he'd made good headway, I took a step back and let him lead the life he'd built for himself. I went back to Faerie for a while, where your grandfather employed me. But since time is odd between the places and time wasn't one of my elements, when I returned, Arthur had aged, and I was the same as I've always been.

"That romantic nonsense with Lancelot and Guinevere was fully fictional. Arcturus was too busy to marry. He wasn't the kind of king to sit on a throne and enjoy luxuries. He was in a saddle, leading men. He did die because he was betrayed, but it was to an enemy who knew the sheath protected him. The enemy sent in a medieval Mata Hari, who stole the sheath. When Arthur was wounded in battle, he couldn't heal."

He shrugged, but you could still see the pain on his face. He'd loved his adopted son and still missed him.

"I'd just returned to Faerie before this. I should have taken him with me, since he was too old to fight like he used to, but I didn't, and I returned too late. He'd passed before I could get to him." His voice had grown thick with emotion.

I felt a lump grow in my throat. How sad that Arthur had died alone, and his father hadn't made it back to him in time.

Megan had been intent on the story. Once it ended, she hopped off Luke's lap, and approached the enchanter. She reached into her pocket and brought out a magic ball. She whispered her ridiculous magic words, and her sword appeared. She set it on the table in front of Merlin. "Is this the sword?"

He looked up at her and turned back to examine the sword. He picked it up and looked closely at the blade, flipping it over. Nodding, he pointed at some words, his voice thick with emotion. "This says, 'To my son, may he achieve his dreams.'"

Megan nodded. "My life rocks!" She pumped her fist

and gave me a smile, her eyes sparkling. She'd been fighting and practicing with freaking Excalibur.

Merlin handed the sword back, and Megan collapsed it into a ball and shoved it into her pocket.

"What happened to the sheath?" Luke asked. Of course, he focused on the most important part—how to keep Megan safe since she'd decided to be a warrior with a fragile human body.

"It has been lost to history, as I believed the collar to be."

Perhaps the dragons have it in their hoard as well, Mr. Mittens added. I looked sharply at him since he hadn't sent that privately but broadcasted it. He was supposed to keep his nature under wraps.

Merlin didn't seem surprised. He turned to face the cat. "Perhaps. They did enjoy my other enchanted items. Although the sheath wouldn't give them any added help, its use is limited to humans."

Mr. Mittens was plotting something. If it involved the dragons, I hoped he was careful.

I looked at Merlin. Could I trust him? I didn't have a great track record when it came to reading people. My marriage had messed me up, and the experiences with Scott and Sofia had really shaken my confidence. At least now I had a crew I trusted, and they could help me decide if someone was on the up and up.

He had this history with my grandfather, and he was Merlin. The Merlin. That was a hard hump to climb over. But I knew nothing of his motivations. Maybe he wanted the collar back, and Excalibur, now that Megan had shown that hand. Of course, if the sword returned to Dana at Arthur's death, it wasn't Merlin's to take back.

Most importantly, maybe Merlin would be willing to

teach me some more magic. How to enchant was now at the top of my list. And being like me and living on earth, maybe he'd be a better teacher than Dana at some things. I was still shocked that she was the Lady of the Lake from the stories. Wow. That one was hard to deal with.

"What do you know about vampires?" The question surprised me when it burst out of my mouth.

He shrugged. "They aren't my favorites."

Megan barked out a laugh, and then choked on the last bite of her apple. Luke pounded her on the back.

Once she stopped coughing and sputtering, she said, "Join the crowd."

"Why? Are you involved with some?"

"One gave me your phone number. Do you want to explain that?"

Merlin blinked. "I only know one vampire. I met him many years ago and sold some items to him."

"Vic Constantine?"

"Why, yes."

"What is your relationship with him?"

He looked at me, his eyes steady. "Purely business."

"How do we know you aren't here to spy on us?" I asked.

"You called me."

"Yeah, at Vic's insistence."

Merlin shook his head. "I don't know what his reason was, but I barely know him. He had my number because I sold him a few items and potions. Other than that, I couldn't tell you anything about him besides he's a vampire and an old one at that."

"Do you know where he resides?" I asked.

"I know one place, the one I sent the items to. I had no reason or desire to look for any others."

"Would you be willing to share that information?" Gabe asked.

"I don't guarantee client confidentiality, unless I'm paid for it," he answered, although it wasn't really an answer.

"Did he pay for it?" Megan asked.

Merlin smiled a slow smile. I still didn't know if we should trust him. He might be a friend to Ludovic. There was no reason, other than a story about my grandfather, that he'd hitch himself to our wagon.

"No, and frankly I bear no great love to his kind."

Hmpf, was Mr. Mittens' response. I concurred.

We could use Merlin on our side if he was on the up and up and willing. But this time, I'd be smart and do some homework. Time to call Grandpa and ask.

Chapter Twenty-Five

I left Megan, Luke, and Gabe to interrogate Merlin. I wasn't great at it, and I figured my time was best served by fact checking. I called my grandfather on our linked cells. He hadn't been around when we were last there, and I didn't know if he'd answer. But it couldn't hurt to try.

I got lucky. He answered on the sixth ring.

"Brigid, is something wrong?" He hadn't learned that phone etiquette was to say "hello."

"Hello, Grandfather. No, nothing is wrong." That wasn't entirely true, but no one was currently attacking us, so this was as good as it got.

"Oh, then I am pleased. I'm sorry I missed your visit."

"Me too." I paused, to make sure the pleasantries were out of the way. He didn't say anything, so I barreled ahead. "I did have a question for you. It is about someone you knew long ago. His name is Merlin or Myrddin."

Silence on the other end.

"Hello, Grandfather, are you still there?" I looked at the

phone. Although the connection was magical, I glanced at my bars. Habit, I supposed.

"Yes, granddaughter, I'm still here. I was just taken aback. I haven't heard that name for years."

"Well, he's here, in my house. He said he knew you of old, and that you were friends with his adopted son, Arcturus."

There was an unidentified sound on his end, maybe a grunt. "I was indeed. Arcturus was a great warrior. I named him my heir once. He's gone from both worlds now."

"Yes." I let the word hang and took a deep breath. "Grandfather, would you consider Merlin trustworthy?"

"If your wishes align with his, I'd say yes. But one thing I learned about him is he has his own agenda. Make sure you know what it is before you trust him."

My heart sank. I didn't know his agenda, and I still wasn't sure about his connection to Vic and the vamps.

"How will I know his agenda?" I said aloud, more to myself than to my grandfather.

"Ask him, he was always truthful to a fault with me."

That was a little reassuring. Having Merlin on our side might turn the tide in our favor, but only if we could trust him. I couldn't imagine a good reason for Vic to give me his number, however. That kept eating at me. Then again, that could be his reason—to keep me mentally unbalanced and untrusting. Or, since he was an evil bastard, to hand me what I wanted and spoil it so I couldn't use it. Was his thinking that convoluted? I didn't know what to think.

"I appreciate the information, Grandfather."

I heard the steward announce something in the background.

"I must go, Brigid, I have visitors coming. I hope you'll come by again soon."

"Yes. I hope to see you as well. Goodbye."

The phone call ended on his side. I put it in my pocket and returned to the kitchen. I could hear Megan asking questions as I entered, so I sat.

Once everyone was done with their conversation, I jumped in, "I called my grandfather."

Merlin's eyebrows shot up. "In Faerie?"

"Yes," I answered.

"You'll have to show me how that is done someday."

I nodded. That wasn't a big deal, and it might be the impetus to convince the enchanter to teach me something.

"I'm going to be blunt, Merlin, he said I should ask you about your agenda. So, I'm going to ask you one thing, straight up and I want a yes or no answer."

He looked at me and waited. I took a deep breath.

"Do you have any current involvement with any vampire, now or planned for in the future, who is associated with Ludovic Constantine?"

He looked me straight in the eye. "No."

"Are you under any geas or oath to any vampire?"

"No."

"Do you have any plans or are considering any that have to do with me, my friends, or family or anything we own or possess?"

"Yes."

I blinked. "What is it?"

"That's not a yes or no question, now is it?" he asked with a twinkle in his eye.

I sighed.

"I plan to find out more about you and your abilities."

"Why?"

He shrugged. "Curiosity."

"Would you be willing to help us win our current war with the vamps?"

"Maybe. I'll think about it."

A bugle in the backyard ended my interrogation. Goch bugled a lot, but it was usually because he was either excited, scared, or warning us. We all jumped up and headed towards the back door. Merlin looked confused.

"Was that a dragon?" he asked.

No one answered, we were all out the door.

Goch was in the middle of the parking lot, waiting for us.

I did it, Mr. Mittens! he announced to all of us.

Mr. Mittens jumped up on the banister of the back porch, his favorite perch.

You did? Let's see it, Mr. Mittens said drolly.

Goch shifted a few feet to the right to reveal an object on the ground he must have been carrying in his talons. Mr. Mittens leapt down, trotted over, and sniffed the object, batting it with his paw.

Merlin, is this the right one? he asked.

We all hurried over and stood in a half circle around it. Goch watched overhead, nearly dancing with excitement.

Merlin reached down and plucked the long object up. It was a sword sheath. It was blackened with age, but it was encrusted with gems and gold accents. Although the leather of the scabbard was cracked and weathered, it still looked in amazing condition considering its great age.

He examined it closely, and I could feel the pulse of Fae magic as he did something to identify it.

He held it out towards Megan. "My lady, it is the sheath to your sword."

Megan moved tentatively to touch it, pausing inches away. "Is it mine?"

"It's not mine to give," Merlin said. "I didn't make it, and I've never owned it."

She looked up at Goch. If his face could form a smile, he'd be grinning ear to ear. He looked at Mr. Mittens.

I did what you said, and they said yes!

Mr. Mittens turned his face to Megan. *The dragons have gifted it to you.*

Megan looked between the cat and the dragon. "Thank you! Thank you both! I don't know what you did, or what you promised the dragons, but thanks!"

She danced a little jig and stared at the sheath. If it didn't have the added benefit of healing any wounds, it looked like it would be worth a fortune for the jewels alone. Heck, if we could prove the provenance on it, it was beyond priceless. Megan must have realized it at that moment, because she turned a little green.

"This is a historical treasure," she said, unbelieving, then held the sheath out at arm's length like it was a snake about to bite her.

"Uh, what are you doing?" Luke asked her, having watched the whole thing with wide eyes.

"I-I'm not sure what to do," she answered truthfully.

Luckily, my cat, who had apparently arranged the whole thing said, *Hmpf. You wear it.*

We laughed a little, and Megan turned pink. She unwound the belt that was wrapped about it, revealing even more splendor, and wrapped it around her waist. She stood still for a moment, then gasped. I jumped.

"What's wrong?"

She pulled up her sleeve and looked at her elbow. "I felt a tingle. Look! My arm is healed!"

She'd scraped her elbow the day before on a nail

sticking out of the fence at the dairy. I'd seen the mark, and it was completely gone.

"It healed me," she said in wonder. "It's like one of Dana's healing balls on steroids!"

"Well, she did make it," I mumbled.

I was grateful, but at the same time, I knew the dragons didn't just hand over this kind of treasure for nothing. I gave my cat the side eye. "What did you do?"

He gave me a slow blink. *I promised them Merlin.*

Chapter Twenty-Six

I wanted to scream at my cat, but I didn't need Merlin to hear this. We could communicate silently, but I didn't think I could keep my emotions off my face. "We're going to go in the house, and when we're alone, you're going to start at the beginning and tell me what you promised exactly."

As you wish, he said. He liked to pull out movie lines when he knew I was mad.

"You aren't going to *Princess Bride* your way out of this one," I scolded, even if I laughed a little on the inside.

He stood and shook his floof out. He walked casually up to the porch and entered through the back door.

Goch was happy, and since the kid needed praise, I thanked him and told him what a great thing he'd done. Whatever part he'd played in this, I knew the mastermind was my cat. I couldn't be mad at the dragon, he'd do anything to please Mr. Mittens, particularly after the hunting incident.

Goch brought his head down to my level. I used my knuckles to give him a good scratch between the eyes.

"Were the other dragons nicer this time?" I asked him.

They were the same, but my mother chastised them good. They promised to be nicer.

"That's good." I scratched again. "You know, if you want to go home, we won't think less of you."

He was quiet. *I know, Brigid. I'm not ready. I think I want to change things in dragon society, but I need to learn more. I'll go back someday. Don't worry about me.*

He sounded more mature and grown up. He'd be a great leader someday. I gave him another pat, nodded to Merlin, and headed in. Megan and Luke were talking to Merlin, and he seemed fascinated with Goch. Gabe caught up to me, and together, we went to talk to Mr. Mittens.

Mr. Mittens jumped up on the table. *Pet*, he started. If he thought that I'd think he was cute, and he'd get out of this, he was mistaken. *I didn't offer anything we cannot provide easily.*

"What was it?"

They want another enchanted object. Something made by Merlin.

I rolled my eyes, he was deliberately avoiding the question, hoping I'd be put off by vague answers. I tapped my foot.

"You aren't answering me."

The object is not important. It doesn't matter. You just need to convince Merlin to make it. He flicked his tail and held me with his blue-eyed stare.

"I can't if I don't know what it is."

He sat down and curled his tail around his feet. He was doing aristocratic cat. He gave a small kitty sigh. *It is nothing, a trifle. But you will be angry if I tell you. You get the enchanter to agree. I'll tell him.*

That made me nearly apoplectic. "No."

He spluttered. *No? Whyever not?*

I took a deep breath and counted silently to ten. I sat down and folded my hands in my lap. I was not going to get mad. He'd made sure Megan was protected. Protector was his job. I needed to let it go. But if my cat was promising things he could not deliver, I needed to know.

Softly, I repeated. "What is it?"

Fine, he said. *They want a golden crown to match the collar.*

"OK, why would that make me mad?"

They want it to do the same things that the collar does.

"They want a crown that will enslave another being?"

I suppose, they didn't say, they said it needed to be the same. I didn't ask in case they didn't know.

"And you are fine with that?"

He licked a piece of fur that had become dislodged from its spot. *I would not allow such a thing to touch me. But I am not going to judge their intent.*

That made me think. Was I judging someone else by my own morals? I balked a bit. Yes, I was. But at the same time, I didn't want to be the reason someone else was *enslaved*. I didn't know the reason they needed the crown either or have any reason to believe they'd misuse it. They hadn't misused the collar.

Once I trusted Merlin more, I was going to have him permanently disable the slave function. I huffed to myself. Merlin himself had said the dragons didn't know about it. Anyway, it was my fault it was active again.

Maybe I was being ridiculous. I just had to ask, or Mr. Mittens did. If Merlin refused, we might have issues with the dragons, but I'd already fixed the collar. So that had to earn us some grace. However, I still wasn't exactly sure what they'd threatened to do to us if we didn't come through.

"What happens if Merlin refuses?"

My cat laid down and offered his belly to be scratched. I felt like I was being manipulated.

Then we'd better return the sheath quickly?

"Dammit, Mr. Mittens. We can't afford a war with the dragons as well as the vamps and the griffins."

You will convince the enchanter or do it yourself. I'm not concerned. He lifted a back paw and groomed it.

Of course he thought that. He was a cat. He only thought ahead to his next meal. Oh well. We had to survive against the vamps first. I'd worry about the rest, later.

"You're asking him."

Hmpf.

He finished his short bath and jumped down, tail swaying. He gave me one backward glance and headed back out to talk to Merlin.

"Well," Gabe said, "For a protector, I think your cat is determined to get us killed."

"Yeah," I said, "Still want to marry me?"

"Is your cat imperious and scary?"

I laughed, "Yes."

"Then, of course I do!"

I walked over to his chair, and he pulled me down into his lap. I wrapped my arms around his neck and let him kiss me until we both were on fire. He stood, still holding me. Laughing, he carried me to the bedroom.

Chapter Twenty-Seven

Merlin left after Mr. Mittens spoke with him. I found out later when I questioned him about what Merlin thought.

He told me Merlin said he'd think about it. Which wasn't reassuring. I didn't need a third war looming over me. But I couldn't do anything about it right now. The gargoyles were coming.

Madison had everything ready for the gargoyles when they started arriving. She'd even planned the festivities for their get together. She was brilliant, and I told her so.

Sam, the leader, was in the first group to arrive. I had a warm spot in my heart for him. He'd bailed us out of trouble with the vamps a couple of times, and I knew he had one agenda—to rid the world of the vampire scourge. Which I was completely on board with.

Brandon, George, and Felicity had been here recently as well. They'd come to help when Megan had been arrested by the police, who were under the control of the vamps. The vamps had taken Megan and tried to put her on a yacht they'd rigged to blow up. Even though we got to

Megan in time, we'd still been lured onto the yacht. Apparently, my time walking ability had saved us. I didn't remember it because in my timeline, it hadn't happened. It was a mind twister. However, while that was going on, Felicity, a lawyer, had gotten the fake charges on Megan dropped.

There were several gargoyles I hadn't met before. Three of them couldn't change into a human form, and so could only come out at night. They were housed in the stable, since their stone forms were too awkward and heavy for the main house.

The first night was just check in and casual dining. Chef Jack had created a buffet style feast in the dining room.

We joined them. I only had five rooms to rent, and a few of the gargoyles were buddying up so that I could house them all for the reunion. Altogether, I had ten staying in the house and three in the stable.

One thing was sure, I didn't have to worry about vamps while the gargoyles were here. The vamps were terrified of the gargoyles. The first time Sam had stayed here, the vamps attacked in numbers to try and take him out of the game. That one gargoyle took out a ton of them. With thirteen gargoyles in residence, we were safe as houses.

I relaxed for the first time in months. This was also my chance to grow the ranks and find more allies for my planned offensive. With the gargoyles, Mr. Mittens at my side, along with the rest of my friends, and Merlin, we had a very good chance of ending this forever.

But tonight? I could sit, enjoy the company of my companions, and listen to the gargoyles tell us their story. Ever since I'd first met them, and Sam had declared that gargoyles were made to eradicate the vampires, I'd been dying to hear the tale.

We filled our plates, and Megan, Luke, Madison, Gabe, Mr. Mittens, and I settled in to listen.

Sam had a gift for storytelling, it so happened.

"Long ago, the vampires were multiplying so fast, that humanity was in danger of being overrun and destroyed utterly," he began. We all leaned in. "There was a great conclave of church leaders and magic users of all kinds, and the leader of the group, someone who you might know." He paused for a drink of water, and we stabbed him with our eyes.

"A great man of art and science, Leonardo da Vinci." We gasped. He had a true grasp of drama. "He isn't as well known for his sculptures, since he didn't enjoy them as much as his drawings and paintings, but he came up with an idea to destroy the vampires through the use of a series of grotesques. He'd sculpt monsters in the form of church gargoyles to fight vampires and other nasty supernatural monsters. His idea was to fuse the clay sculptures with the soul of a willing warrior and give them the ability to fight at night in a nearly impervious stone form that would possess abilities equal to the vampires themselves.

"The magic users agreed to bring the sculptures to life, and the church leaders helped seal the souls into the final creation. Then came the search for willing warriors. It was difficult to expect current warriors to lay down their lives so their souls might be used, so the magic users that were gifted with necromancy, searched for souls still loose on the earth. And they found plenty of angry warriors willing to go into battle again."

"Who were they?" Megan asked, although I knew her knowledge of history to be limited, if it didn't have to do with some great drama.

Sam smiled, and I knew he was about to blow our socks off. "I was once known as Alexander the Great."

I blinked. The room grew really quiet. We looked at each other. It made sense. Sam was quite handsome, although I'd assumed he'd be blond, not dark-haired. He had light green eyes and was stockily built and strong looking. Now that I knew his identity, I looked up the images of statues of Alexander, and the resemblance was uncanny.

"Wasn't Alexander blond?" I blurted out.

Sam laughed. "I am a natural strawberry blond. I dye my hair each time I change identities. Sam feels like a brunette." He shrugged. "I get bored."

So, Sam was vain and adventurous.

"OK."

"Any others we'd know?" Megan insisted. I figured she knew who Alexander the Great was.

"Some, I'm sure, although unless you are a student of military history, probably not all. I'll list the ones I know you've heard of." He took another drink. "I'm in some great company and most are also great leaders, but they've elected to keep me in charge for now." He pointed to George.

I'd met George when we rescued Megan. He was taller than Alexander, still stocky like a warrior, muscular, with short dark hair, Asian features, and unique eyes. Not brown, more amber colored, and light-colored skin with a ruddy tint. I had no idea who he was.

"George here was once known as Genghis Khan."

There was another gasp from all of us. George smiled and winked at me. He was cheeky, that was for sure. Of course, wasn't he known for liking a lot of women?

Sam went on, "Felicity, who you've met, was a great

warrior, although she chooses to fight our other battles now. Her name was once Cynane, and she is my sister."

Sister? That was cool. Two great warriors in one family. I didn't know her, and I'd have to look her up later as well.

He went through and gave the other ten warriors' names. I knew some and had no idea on others. "Saladin, Hannibal Barca, Boudicca, William Wallace, Zenobia, Sun Tzu, Leonidas, Richard the Lionheart, Godfrey of Bouillon, and Adhemar Le Puy. We are a bit heavy on crusaders, since the church was involved." There were a few eye rolls from his fellow gargoyles at that statement. "We are the few that are in North America. Altogether, a total of seven hundred and seventy-seven of us were made. A sacred number to the church."

So many. But only a fraction of the number of vamps, I assumed. We'd killed hundreds of them, and that was just the ones in this area. I figured Vic would be pulling in more from other places.

"We've lost a few over the years, and our number has fallen below five hundred, but we are still strong, and sure of our mission," Sam finished.

The other gargoyles made gestures to say they agreed.

"Vampires have been a scourge on humanity long enough," George said. "We battled them in life; we continue to battle them in our second lives."

"Those stories would make the history books more interesting," Megan said under her breath. If things weren't so surreal, I'd laugh at that.

"So, after they chose you, and your spirits responded, then what happened?" Gabe asked, enthralled by the story. He always liked history, so I assumed he knew the people I didn't recognize.

"After we agreed, the magicians and church leaders

sealed us in the now animate grotesques that Leonardo had sculpted. Those bodies became our own. Luckily, most of us could shift into our original forms during the day and live a partial human life again. Unfortunately, that didn't work for us all." He smiled warmly at the three in gargoyle form. The three didn't react, but their eyes flicked to him.

"We scattered over the world and began our hunt. Our goal is to end every vampire, but although we made a serious dent in them, they reproduce so quickly, it is a difficult goal. Especially with our numbers dwindling. That is why we agree to team up with any who take on the task as well." He looked me in the eye.

I blushed. I didn't want to take on the world of vampires, and I said so. "Sam, my goal is to get rid of the vampires here, in Kilchis. We appreciate your help in doing so, but I can't go beyond that."

He nodded. "We understand. One master vamp is worth thousands even up to millions of new vamps, any chance we get to eliminate one, we take it. Don't worry."

"Thanks."

"We do have a boon to ask of you."

My blood ran cold.

He looked at the collar I wore.

"That is the Golden Collar of Merlin, is it not?"

My throat was tight. I nodded, my hand grasping it involuntarily. I couldn't give it to them or even lend it; it wasn't mine.

"We assume that you know of him. I ask that you put us in touch."

A flicker of irritation joined my feeling of impending doom. Knowing Merlin was becoming more trouble than he was worth.

Chapter Twenty-Eight

"I do know him. I'll let him know you wish to speak to him, but I can't guarantee he will," I answered. My throat was still tight. We couldn't afford to lose the gargoyles' help. What if this small thing was the reason they bailed on us?

"That is all we can ask," Sam said.

Since I had zero control over what Merlin did, the relief that washed through me almost took me to the ground. I was lucky we were sitting. Gabe noticed though, and his hand rested on mine in my lap. Mr. Mittens leaned against me, and I steadied.

"Good, because we have a plan, and we were hoping you'd be willing to go along with it," I said.

Sam's eyes brightened and the intensity of all the gargoyles' eyes landing on me was a physical weight.

"We are going to attack the vamps on their home soil and wipe them out for good."

"Do you know where they are?"

"Not yet, but we are looking. We have a few ideas that need to be checked out."

The gargoyles looked at each other. Felicity spoke up. "We have some ideas as well; we should share."

"Yes, we'll take any intel you have," I responded.

Felicity leaned in. "They've abandoned the warehouse near the bay, and it appears as though they are setting up a warehouse in Lincoln City about fifty miles south of you."

"So, still fairly close?"

"It appears so. Of course, we've got someone watching to see if Vic Constantine is also staying close by, but we do know that Bella has been seen a lot, supervising the move."

Hmpf, Mr. Mittens interjected. *If we don't get the master, it won't matter.* He jumped up on my lap so he could face the crowd. He licked a paw, dismissing everyone.

He was right.

Gabe leaned forward. "Has anyone seen if Vic has been going overseas or traveling outside of the area? We think he's exhausted his supply of old vamps, and we decimated the sea of young vamps he threw at us a few weeks ago. He has to pull in vampires from elsewhere or build more newbies."

Sam was shaking his head. "His true base before he came to America was in Romania. He'll have to go there— if he hasn't already—and get the help of the ancient vamps he left behind to rule there. Trust me, he's got vamps at the ready, and once they get here, he'll throw them all at you. I don't know if he's left recently, or sent an email, but they are coming."

I shivered. Dammit. I was hoping his troops were wiped out, but it looked like just his American ones were. We needed to attack now, before his reinforcements arrived.

"Well, that news just moved up our time frame. We can't afford for more old vamps to come," I said.

"It might be too late," Felicity added. "The movement

to the new site could be corresponding with their arrival. He needed a bigger facility for his troops. He wouldn't want them loose in his territory."

My heart sank. I clutched Gabe's hand tightly, and Mr. Mittens went stiff. That made too much sense. Otherwise, why abandon their current headquarters? They might suspect but they couldn't know we were going to go on the offensive.

"That isn't what I wanted to hear, but it makes sense." I wanted to scream in frustration.

Just as I finished talking, I felt the warm pulse of realm walking magic and turned to stare at the door leading to the dining room. Merlin strode through. He smiled and waved at me, then helped himself to a plate and started to fill it. I looked at him with a frown. Had I invited him and forgot?

"I invited him," Megan whispered after seeing my face. "He should help, and he needs to meet the gargoyles."

"OK."

After his plate was full, he headed over.

"I'd like you all to meet Merlin."

The gargoyles' heads moved as one to stare.

"I guess you are now in touch with him," I followed up lamely and smiled.

Sam stood up and approached him. "I'm Sam, the gargoyle leader. It's a great pleasure to meet you. We have some questions if you don't mind."

Merlin waved to his food, "Sure, if you don't mind if I eat first."

"No, no, carry on!" He sat back down, and Merlin dug in, glancing up once in a while as he followed along in the conversation.

We only talked for a little while longer, because without true intel, we were just guessing. Sam agreed to send a crew over later tonight to check out the situation. Their reunion festivities were starting in the morning, so it was the ideal time. The human gargoyles were able to shift and fly at night without being immobilized by the sun. The non-human gargoyles were trapped inside during the day if they wanted to move, since their stone forms were mobile as long as the sun didn't touch them.

I did ask Sam how their magic worked. He explained they were made like that so they could watch from the churches of their time easily. They were fully aware when frozen in stone by the sun. I found that sort of disturbing. Being frozen and aware. But he glossed over it. Since those able to shift lived human lives during the day, I got the feeling they also didn't enjoy the sensation.

Once Merlin was finished eating, I stood and signaled to my friends to leave so the gargoyles could speak to him alone about their own business.

Chapter Twenty-Nine

I went to bed, so I didn't stay up to see what happened on the gargoyle's reconnaissance mission. But it was the first thing I wanted to hear once I woke. Gabe had already left for work, and Megan was training with the baincapall when I wandered out for breakfast.

Sam was alone in the dining room, and I grabbed crepes and eggs before I sat down with him. Mr. Mittens was eating his meal in the kitchen, then heading out to hunt for Brightfeather and her chicks.

I sat down next to Sam. "How did you sleep?"

He blinked. "I rested well."

"Any news?" I really wanted an update on their talk with Merlin, but that was their business. Most importantly, I wanted to know if they found the vamp lair.

He smiled. "Yes, it appears to be the lair. I think we can plan."

I squirmed a little. "Any old vamps?" This was my real worry, that we were too late, and the battle would be serious.

He frowned. "Yes, it appears that at least ten of his lieutenants from Romania have joined him with many of their young."

My shoulders slumped. That was the worst news. I sighed and ate a bite of my breakfast which now tasted like ash. I swallowed and pushed the plate away. I'd lost my appetite. "Any guesstimate on total numbers?"

"Yeah, we have a good idea. I'd say from what we observed, two to three hundred new vamps."

"Well, crap."

He smiled. "I agree, but the new vamps aren't as hard to dispatch, so that's a bonus."

I nodded, but I wasn't feeling quite as optimistic. The gargoyles were worth several vamps, I had the new exploding fireballs, the werewolves, the baincapall, my power, and Mr. Mittens. I could probably ask Goch to join. I refused to risk Brightfeather right now. Gabe was good and could heal himself, and now that Megan had the sheath to Excalibur, she was also gonna be hard to kill. My ally game was strong. Too bad the vamps had a game that was equally strong.

I thanked him and scraped my plate into the trash. Madison had the festivities in hand, and I was needed elsewhere. I considered slipping to Faerie to gather more allies, but that would incur more debts. My grandfather might help, but I hated to ask him since he was so busy. I guess my best bet was to practice using the collar with Mr. Mittens so we knew how much it could hold and how much we'd both need. I'd have to wait for him to get back, though.

"Brigid!" I turned to see who was calling me.

One of the new baincapall guards was at the kitchen door. I walked towards her.

"Yes?"

"I was sent to get you. There is trouble at the dairy."

"Is it vampires?"

She shrugged. "We captured a spy."

If it wasn't a vamp, what was it? I guess I'd wait until I got there. The new guard wasn't very talkative. Probably because she was down the ladder in the hierarchy.

I followed her out, her lanky seven-foot form shading me from the infrequent sun. I hurried along to keep up with her ground-eating stride.

Megan was already there, having been training with the others. We crossed through the woods and across the first pasture. Milk Dud was running around, his new mother watching him fondly and grazing peacefully. I grinned at them, happy we could help both sad creatures. I could see the baincapall—Megan small next to them—in the open area outside of the fenced pasture. I wasn't close enough to see who they'd captured, because they had whoever it was surrounded.

We exited through the gate and joined the throng. I stumbled when I saw the griffin standing in the center. Griffins were fierce. The adults were the size of a draft horse with immense wings, sharp killing talons, and equally sharp beaks. This one stood calmly, even with several baincapall spears pointed at it. My heart sank. If the griffins were spying, they could have discovered Brightfeather's secret. I swallowed hard.

Megan backed out of the circle and put her spear back into her pocket after collapsing it into a magic ball. She pulled me aside.

"This isn't good. The griffin hasn't said anything, but it only landed because Goch forced it down here. Goch said he caught it near the nest."

"Dammit."

"Yeah, it said it will only speak to its masters, I'm assuming the king and queen."

"Probably."

"What are we going to do? The second it goes back, the jig is up," she finished.

I sighed. This was the worst thing that could happen. Sure, I was hoping we could figure this out and that the royals would be happy to know about their grandchildren, but if they found out from a spy, they'd be angry. This was going to force our hand one way or the other. Either I had to spirit away Brightfeather and her babies to Faerie or confront the griffins now. It was time to talk to Brightfeather. I didn't know how well she'd respond to this added stressor. She'd been on her last nerve for a while. Poor thing.

I'd have to go talk to her. We couldn't let this griffin go until we knew what he knew, and since he wasn't talking, the only way to know, was to give Brightfeather the choice about what to do with him. I sighed again and told Megan I'd go talk to her, then I walked.

Mr. Mittens was leaving the nest as I appeared. He blinked, surprised.

Is something wrong, pet? he asked.

"Yes, we found a griffin spy. There's a good chance he flew over the nest."

Mr. Mittens froze. *The chicks haven't been out. There's no way he'll know.* At least someone was thinking logically.

"I sure hope not, but he's not speaking, and I need to warn Brightfeather."

As you wish. He followed me back into the nest.

"Brightfeather, we're coming back in," I warned. I was always careful not to startle the protective mother griffin.

Brigid, it is lovely to see you! she said as soon as I turned the corner. My little namesake cheeped loudly and bounced, flapping her wings. They'd all grown some more, and it'd only been a few days since I'd visited. They still looked scruffy—half baby fluff, half new feathers—their lion halves were also starting to look patchy as they began to shed their baby fuzz.

"I'm happy to see you too, my friend, but I have bad news."

Her head shot up, and she went from relaxed to alert in a flash. *What is it?* she asked, her mental voice strained.

"The baincapall have captured a griffin spy. He was initially caught by Goch who said he was flying over your nest."

This time she stood quickly, startling the chicks, who erupted into squeaks and ruffled feathers. She gathered them protectively with her wings. *Oh no*, her mental voice was a whisper, the horror reflected in it was a gut punch. *What are we going to do?* Her eyes pleaded with me.

I swallowed hard and looked her in the eye. "It's time to make the hard choice. We preempt the spy, and you tell the king and queen, or you flee to Faerie. My grandfather will protect you."

Chapter Thirty

Little Brigid broke free of her mom and threw herself at me. I gathered her up, she was almost too big to hold anymore, and her long limbs dangled as I clutched her to my chest. I stroked her baby soft fuzz, which was now intermixed with harder feathers. I lowered my head and kissed the top of hers.

I don't know what to do, Brightfeather said. I could feel her anguish like it was tangible.

I wished I could make the choice for her, but it wasn't something I could do. I could offer one thing though. Protection. No matter what her choice, I'd protect the babies and my friend. I straightened my shoulders.

"If you want to talk to your in-laws, we'll all go with you and keep you safe. We can leave the children in Faerie and go."

She blinked a few times, looked at the chicks, and then back at me. *Yes.* That single word seemed to give her strength, and she continued, *You are right. It's time to tell them and to take back control, even if it means I die.*

I choked. "I will not let you die. We will realm walk out if that's the only choice they give us."

She nodded, sadly, but I could see she believed it was a possibility.

"Do you want us to take the chicks to Faerie?"

She gave one bob of her head.

"OK. I'll do that first, then we'll go." I looked at my cat. "Call Goch while I'm gone and see if he'll go with us to the griffins. We'll need to take as many people as he can carry."

As you wish.

He stepped and vanished, the pulse of his magic punching through me.

I waited until Brightfeather had caressed each of her chicks and spoke to them, then they gathered around me, the two males clutching my clothing with their beaks. With little Brigid back in my arms, I walked.

I stepped into my grandfather's den, and he gaped at me in shock.

"Sorry, Grandfather, I didn't have time to call."

He folded his arms. "What is this?"

"I have a bit of a situation. I was hoping that I could leave the griffin chicks here for a day or so. They are really sweet, if a bit rambunctious."

To punctuate that, little Brigid gave a sharp cheep and buried her little face in my armpit. I stroked her as her brothers trembled against my legs.

"Their mother, my friend Brightfeather, is in a spot of trouble, and I'm trying to help her out. Either it'll work out and I'll come get them, or it won't, and they'll need to seek refuge with you. If you don't mind." I probably should have talked to him about this before dumping it on him, but I was hoping it wouldn't come to this.

He approached slowly, his hands out. "I didn't think I'd ever see griffins in Faerie again."

It was my turn to be surprised. "Griffins are Faerie creatures?"

"They were once, but they left long ago for other realms."

That made me curious. Why had they left? I'd have to ask sometime when I had the headspace for it. Now, I needed to stay focused on my current problems.

Grandfather stroked a hand down Brigid's feathers, and she slowly relaxed. He knelt and stroked little Umber and Brightstorm as well until all the griffin babies were relaxed and comfortable with him.

"They eat raw meat," I warned him.

He nodded. But now he was sitting cross-legged, and three large chicks were trying to all sit in his lap at once. He laughed.

I pointed to each chick and told him their names.

"What trouble did their mother get into?" he asked, casually.

"Umm, the royal kind?" I said uncertainly. I wasn't sure if this was the time and place to spill Brightfeather's business. If they had to come live here, I'd do it then.

He nodded, knowingly. "Don't worry, I'll watch over them until you return, and yes, Faerie would be proud if griffins wish to return."

I threw my arms around his neck and kissed his cheek. "You are the best, Grandfather." I almost thanked him but stopped in time. "I'll be back soon, either way."

He patted my arm, and I gave each chick a parting pet and walked.

I stepped back into the nest. Brightfeather waited for me. I offered to walk her to the house, but she wanted to fly, so I walked back. Mr. Mittens, Goch, and Megan were there waiting for me, so at least my cat had succeeded finding Goch quickly.

"Brightfeather is flying, did Mr. Mittens fill you in?" I asked as I approached.

"Yeah," Megan added.

"What did you do with the spy?" I asked.

"Sorcha had him tied up and tossed into a stall."

I frowned.

"He's a little butt hurt, but not physically hurt," Megan added. "What's the plan?"

"We're backup. I don't know what Brightfeather is going to say, but she seems to think they'll kill her for it, so if things look iffy, we grab her and realm walk out. Since everyone except you can realm walk, I'm hoping we can get out unscathed."

"Well, I'm armed. And we're taking a dragon and a killer cat. You're expecting a fight."

I nodded. "I am. I don't want one, because I don't think we can win against the griffins, but I'll do whatever we have to do to save Brightfeather."

"Even if it starts another war?"

"Just so you know, I've left everything to you. If I have to flee to Faerie for good, the paperwork is in my office."

"Don't be ridiculous. You'd have to come back and pack and get Gabe." She gave me a goofy grin. She knew I couldn't leave without saying goodbye.

"True, we'll talk about it then. But if it all goes sideways, it's best if I'm gone so the vamps and the griffins will leave you alone."

"I go where you go." Her jaw was set. Stubborn Megan was hard to deal with.

"We'll fight about it later." I could just refuse to realm

walk her to Faerie. Of course, she had Goch, so there was that. A problem for later.

I could hear wingbeats and looked up. Brightfeather's silver feathers shone in the light. I sent Gabe a quick text, hopefully one that wouldn't worry him too much. Megan had already put the harness on Goch, so Megan, Mr. Mittens and I climbed aboard. I'd ordered an additional harness for Mr. Mittens so he could dragon ride without flying off. Without further fanfare, Goch leapt into the air, his mighty wings beating with the effort of his climb, and we followed Brightfeather to our possible doom.

Chapter Thirty-One

I didn't bother casting my shadow magic over us. For whatever reason, Goch said it was his natural magic, people refused to notice a griffin and a bright red dragon flying overhead. Except for one really persistent fighter pilot. She'd followed us from Kilchis through the mountains to Portland before she veered off. She'd gotten close enough that we knew her call sign was "Screwtop," and she was a woman. I felt uneasy about the whole thing, but she hadn't shot at us, and Megan had given her a friendly wave, which the fighter pilot reluctantly returned.

I didn't like being on the radar of the military, but there wasn't a thing I could do about it now, but not let them know where we'd started from. Then I laughed. What was she going to tell her superiors? She saw a red dragon with riders and a griffin? She'd be thrown out of the military before she finished the statement. I shook my head.

The rest of the flight was uneventful, miles of endless sky, forest and city down below, and the quiet thrump of Goch's leathery wings as he steadily followed the quieter, determined, griffin. I had no idea where we were going. I recognized where we were for a while, but eventually, I lost track as cities and terrain passed us by.

Eventually, Brightfeather's voice filled my head. *We are nearly there, be cautious.* She began to glide, and Goch joined her as we descended slowly like a big airliner.

There was endless forest below us and rolling mountains, but no settlement or city that I could see. I strained to see our destination, but it wasn't clear where we were going.

Suddenly, we passed through what felt like ice water, and I shivered hard. And there below us was a white stone city.

We've passed through the ward to the Invisible City, Brightfeather announced.

I felt a wave of dismay. I'd never asked her about her home. I was a terrible friend. I assumed they lived in caves like the dragons, but this was as complex as any human city. I gazed in wonder. A white stone city lay sprawled below us. We were aiming towards the largest building on the crest of a hill. The palace, I assumed. Sure enough, Brightfeather circled the building and spiraled in for a landing. The landing area was very large, like a helipad for a jetliner, so Goch had no problem following her and finding a spot to land without squishing anything vital on the ground.

The architecture was reminiscent of Faerie, partially confirming my new knowledge that griffins had once lived in Faerie. Before we could dismount, we were surrounded by guards. Brightfeather moved to intercept them. Once they recognized her, they backed away but still barred us from moving closer to anyone but Goch.

"What do you think they're going to do?" Megan asked.

"I don't know. I guess we wait."

Mr. Mittens leaned casually against my legs, ready to jump anyone that came near. The griffins ignored him, misreading him as the least dangerous member of our party, and kept a wary eye on the giant red dragon, who was gentler than a kitten, at least an *Earth* kitten.

We waited as Brightfeather conversed with an imperious-looking guard, who eventually moved off.

Brightfeather approached us. *Flamemane went to announce us.*

"Will they meet us out here or inside?" I asked, concerned that if we had to go in, we'd lose the benefit of having Goch with us.

Her eyes flicked to Goch. *No, they will come out, because my guest can't enter.*

So, the griffins still had the Fae guesting laws embedded in their culture.

"Good." I looked her over, trying to gauge her level of anxiety. She seemed strangely calm. I guess she knew this was the deciding moment and didn't have the head space left to worry. Either that, or she was a lot more settled than I would have been in her place.

Brigid, promise me you'll care for my babies? she asked suddenly.

I froze. My heart sank. She wasn't calm, she was resigned to a terrible fate. I wanted to hug her, comfort her.

"I will raise them as if they were my own, but let's find a way out of this, before we think of that."

She gave a quick nod, but her eyes were still resigned.

We waited quietly, but as we did, I noticed something I hadn't when we first arrived. I felt Fae magic. It was slight, unlike the constant current I could feel on my land, but somewhere here, there was a small link to Faerie. I looked around as though I could see such a thing. Even on my land, knowing where the link was, there wasn't any way to see it. It was just a spot where pure magic flowed into my land and kept it filled. This link wasn't that impressive. It might fill a room or a small building, but it wouldn't fill acres like my link did.

That gave me the start of an idea. I let it percolate in the back of my mind. Something to maybe bargain with if things went south.

Goch shifted, and since I'd been leaning on him, I almost lost my balance.

Sorry, Brigid, he said into my mind. *Do you think they'll come back soon? My scales itch under the harness.*

"Where Goch? I'll see if I can scratch it for you."

Megan has to do it, only her spear is strong enough for a good scratch, he remarked.

I looked at Megan. She'd been listening, so she moved to grab her magic ball with her spear to give Goch a scratch.

I held up a hand. "I don't think pulling out a weapon in hostile territory is a good idea."

She dropped her hands. "Yeah, I didn't think that one through."

She apologized to Goch, who tried to reach his itch with a back claw.

It's OK, he said. *I don't want to make things worse for Bright-feather.*

"Yeah, that's right," Megan said out loud and patted his side.

After what felt like an hour, but was probably more like forty minutes, several guards exited the palace into the courtyard where we waited, followed by the king and queen. The times I'd met the king and queen before, they'd been free of any adornment but their guards. This time, they both wore golden collars, not that unlike mine in shape. However, they didn't have an overlarge central jewel like mine did. These were intricately adorned and sparkled with gems.

As they approached, I straightened up, on high alert, and stood next to Brightfeather. I put a comforting hand on her neck and sent a reassuring mental message to her. Her muscles were tense under the thick, soft feathers of her neck.

"You got this," I whispered as the entire entourage stopped and parted to allow the king and queen to approach.

I dropped my hand, and she took one step forward and bowed to her royal in-laws. We followed suit. I dropped into my best court curtsy.

To what do we owe the pleasure, near daughter? the queen asked. *I believe you still have time to help your friend, do you not?*

I do, your majesty, but I have come on a different matter altogether. Brightfeather appeared utterly miserable.

It must be important indeed for you to look so out of sorts, the queen responded.

It is the most important thing in all the world to me. She shifted on her feet. *Before I explain it to you, I beg a boon.*

The queen looked surprised. Which was hard to do when you didn't have eyebrows, but her head tilted ever so slightly to the right. *Of course, my daughter, what do you desire?*

Brightfeather was quiet a beat. *I desire that you hear my entire story before you cast judgment upon me and seek my destruction.*

Destruction? That is a harsh judgment. I do not think we need to go that far. I will grant the boon.

Brightfeather dipped her head in acknowledgement,

took a deep breath, letting it out slowly, and started her tale.

Umber, my Umber, came back to me, she started. *As you know, we had a rough start, but like the great-hearted griffin that he was, he chose to do right by me.*

The king gazed off into the clouds, I could tell he was deeply affected by the loss of his son, so much so he didn't trust himself to speak. The queen, however, gazed at Brightfeather with kindness and perhaps love.

I was reluctant. He'd hurt me, and I'd left determined to live a life apart from society. I was surprised when he came back to me. Surprised, but happy. We truly wanted to build a life together, to start over, and we'd begun to, when he was suddenly killed.

Her mental voice caught. She was speaking out loud to the griffins, but keeping up her mental translation for us, for which I was grateful.

The queen was now looking away, sorrow reflecting in her eyes. This family had lost so much. Surely, they'd be fools to condemn the remaining member to death.

I didn't know that I bore his eggs until later.

Both king and queen swung their heads at her in shock.

I was blessed with three healthy chicks. Umber, for his father, Brightstorm for mine, and Brigid, for my friend. They grow healthy and strong, and they are cared for greatly by my friends and myself. I was not ready to share them with anyone. I've been deep in grief, and in doing so, I broke our laws. I have come to confess. I hope that your love for Umber will spare my life.

She stopped speaking and bowed until her beak touched the ground and stayed there as though expecting an immediate blow.

The royals were in shock. They stood silent for a long time.

Where are they? the queen finally demanded. She cast

around as though we'd brought the chicks with us and were hiding them from her.

I stepped forward. "They are safe, your majesty. We need to know they will remain so before we present them to you."

Brightfeather remained in her subservient position.

We would never harm our grandchildren. They are royal heirs. She sounded as imperious as she appeared.

I felt the hair raise on my neck. We needed her compassion, not her royal affront.

"What of your daughter, their mother?" I continued.

Our laws are clear, she must die, the queen declared.

Chapter Thirty-Two

Everything happened at once. The guards snapped to attention and started to approach. Megan whipped out her sword and shield, Goch raised his head and bugled, and Mr. Mittens went from docile fuzzy housecat to his Splintercat form in a breath. I moved another step forward, so I was in front of Brightfeather.

"We do not wish to make enemies of the griffins, who we hold in high esteem, but we will if you attempt to kill our friend," I announced clearly so all could hear.

The griffin guards spread their wings partially and expanded as their feathers fluffed outward, giving them a very terrifying sense of size. It didn't take much to make them scarier than they already were. Their sharp beaks and deadly talons were frightening enough. I swallowed but stood my ground. I knew we could disappear in an instant if we had too, and I was within reach of Brightfeather so she'd go with us.

"Brightfeather might be resigned to her fate, but I have the chicks. I will keep them and your daughter if you follow

169

through with that horrible decision. I suggest we discuss this like civilized beings before any rash decisions are made on either side."

The queen cocked her head at me, but it was the king who responded.

We will not be dictated to by insignificant humans! he roared, and the guards all took a step inward.

Mr. Mittens stood next to me and bristled, his growl rumbling through my chest and his eyes ablaze. Before this devolved into bloodshed and all options were gone, I needed to do something. I straightened to my full height and gathered my power. Careful not to singe anyone, I encircled my group with a ring of fire and shouted back at the king.

"I'm no human. I am Fae!"

The king, his owlish eyes already large, stared straight into me.

Tricks! The Fae left this place long ago.

My fire wasn't impressive enough. I needed another trick to make this work. I called the air, and I felt it whip my hair about as I commanded it to mix with the fire, taking the flames higher, until they resembled a whirlwind around us. Before my magic had been returned by Dana, I couldn't have done this. It was stronger than it had been. The guards finally stepped back, some holding their wings over their faces to block the heat. The faint stench of burning feathers rose. Oops.

"Do you need to see more before you believe?" I screamed above the inferno. The guards and the royals stepped back a few more steps.

You are nothing but a cheap magician, the king said.

I wondered why he was doing this. He'd seen us fight the vampires; he'd helped. Hadn't he seen me using my powers then? I thought back. Maybe not. It was hard to see who did what during a battle.

Time to bring out the big guns. I didn't want to hurt anyone, but behind Goch was a tower, and it was in plain view of the important players. While maintaining the ring of fire, I called my most dangerous magic. I raised my hand dramatically, and when I let it fall, I hit the tower with a blast of lightning.

The air around us lit up, the static in the air caused stray hair and loose feathers to rise, and the crack was deafening. Everyone fell silent.

The king looked at me, he was now standing by his mate. His owl eyes huge, and his beak agape.

This cannot be.

"I am the great-granddaughter of the Pendragon to the high king of Faerie," I announced.

Both of the royals appeared stricken.

No, the queen whispered.

I gave them both my harshest look of royal disdain. "Yes, it is so. Now we will speak as equals."

I was pulling that one out of my butt. I had no idea if my minor rank in Faerie was in any way near that of a griffin king or queen, but most of it was the attitude, right?

They stood sullenly and waited.

"You will rescind the order of death. And allow Bright-feather to raise her chicks as she sees fit…" I lifted my hand to silence the protest both royals started to thrust into my mind. "With visiting rights to be determined and appropriate training arranged for when the griffin chicks are old enough for such to begin. And as a gesture of good will, I will increase your link to Faerie, so you may have access to the magic there equal to my link on my homeland."

The royal couple appeared stunned. Then they stared

into each other's eyes, communicating, I assumed. The king stepped forward after they were done. I tried to read their faces, but their bird expressions were impossible.

We will hear terms, he said.

"That is acceptable. I will send the others away, and we can proceed."

I waved Brightfeather and Megan away. Megan protested, but I whispered briefly, "Just go, it'll be fine."

She climbed aboard Goch, and he and Brightfeather sprang into the air and circled, safe for the moment.

Mr. Mittens refused to leave my side. We followed the king and queen into the building. The interior was as immense as the exterior, with ceilings so high, you had to crane your neck to see them, and wide corridors that four griffins could walk comfortably abreast. We walked for a distance before we entered a grand room with griffin-sized cushions. The ceilings were at least twenty feet high, and the walls were covered with murals. The royals seated themselves, so Mr. Mittens and I did as well.

Servants were suddenly everywhere, bringing refreshments and settling in silently to attend to any needs we might have.

We wish to have open visitation with the chicks, the bargaining had begun.

"That is acceptable, as long as we have proper warning about when the visits will occur," I clarified.

There was a nod at a cleric sitting to the side, and the griffin used a talon to mark something on a wax tablet.

We will have the chicks begin their lessons when they have reached a year in age, the queen added.

"That is also acceptable, with the option for Brightfeather to adjust the time within the span of a year."

Six months.

"Done."

Another nod, and the cleric wrote some more.

The chicks will have a guard of four or our best warriors, the king added.

This wasn't something I wanted. I didn't need extra griffins roaming around that I needed to feed.

"No. No guards, the chicks are well-protected."

The king clicked his beak, irritated. *Unacceptable.*

"The chicks are protected by their mother, me, and Mr. Mittens. They are safe."

We will have a member of the royal guard to watch over them, he demanded.

"One."

He nodded, and the scribe recorded it.

As for the expansion of our link to Faerie, when can you have it complete?

"I am embroiled in a war with the vampires, currently, so I require a maximum of one year." I also needed to get help since I didn't have a clue on how to do it. However, Dana did, and I assumed that my grandfather knew how to as well. I just needed time to deal with it.

You expect to take all of these concessions and then not pay your due for a year? The queen sputtered.

"Nine months?" I could probably do all I needed to in six weeks, but I had to make it sound impressive.

"Six."

I almost smiled; Six months was perfect.

"Done," I said and nodded at the cleric, who looked to the king.

He wrote it down.

"I have no other business," I announced and scrambled awkwardly to my feet from the low cushion.

We wish to meet our grandchildren, the queen said softly before I could literally bow out.

"Come tomorrow afternoon," I said firmly. "They'll be ready to meet you." Right after I went to Faerie and brought them back and talked Brightfeather out of the panic attack she'd likely be having.

"I will expect a copy of our agreement when you come," I added, my chin high with my best courtly air. I was faking it so hard it almost hurt, but at the same time I felt proud of my negotiation skills.

Then I marched out with a stiff back and lengthy strides, Mr. Mittens at my side. He hadn't even needed to eat anyone this time.

Once we were free of the door and any spying eyes, I grasped his fur and walked us home before my weak knees and shaking legs gave out.

Chapter Thirty-Three

Thank you, Brigid, thank you so much! Brightfeather said over and over.

I didn't know how to respond to that past a simple, "You're welcome." So that's what I said, but it touched me deeply. It was such a small thing considering all the things she'd done for me, including fighting and risking her own life and the life of her mate, for me. I choked up but didn't have the emotional depth or physical strength to explain to her how much she meant to me.

I left her to go and pick up her babies in Faerie. I walked into grandfather's den to find him rolling around on the floor, playing with the three griffin chicks in a tangle of fun and feathers. They all looked up at me with guilty faces as though they'd been caught being naughty. I laughed and clapped my hands together.

Grandfather stood up, brushed the stray bits of lint, feathers, and fluff off himself and gathered the chicks up. Little Brigid hopped up and down, wiggling to get to me. I held out my arms, and she ran and jumped into them. I had to bend to scoop her the rest of the way, but it was so sweet, and I held her tightly for a time.

"It looks like you had a grand time?" I said, aiming the statement slash question at the chicks and my grandfather.

"We did."

The chicks added in happy trills.

"I'm so glad."

"What happened?" Grandfather asked, once again seated and dignified in his chair by the fire.

"It was touch and go, but we came to an understanding. I'll probably require your assistance to fulfill my part, but we have a buffer of six months. The chicks can go back to their nest for now."

"That's grand, what did you promise them?"

"That I'd expand their link to Faerie," I said a bit sheepishly. I had no idea if it was possible or not. I'd been working on bravado and the one *in* I could see they might go for.

He frowned. "That is a difficult process."

"Is it doable?"

He thought for a moment, then nodded slowly. "I believe that between you, Dana, and me we could do it."

"Good, I'll worry about that later, like I said I gave us some time."

"Yes, we'll need about a month to prepare, so that was good thinking."

"I have to get these babies back, but I..." I wanted to thank him. He stopped me, holding up a hand.

"No need, I accept your gratitude. Now get these rascals home before I decide to keep them."

I smiled, and the two boys clung to my legs as I walked them home to their nest.

When Brightfeather saw them, she lit up. They ran to her, and she gathered them in her wings and held them close. Her eyes were full of love as she looked on me, and I noticed that the weight she'd seemed to bear had fallen away. She looked happier, even her silver feathers were brighter, almost luminous, and my heart filled with joy for her.

"I promised your in-laws a first visit tomorrow. They'll be bringing a copy of all the decisions we made, so we both have it in writing."

Oh, lady Brigid, you don't know what a wonderful thing you've done for us. Thank you.

"You must stop thanking me. You've done more for me than I've ever done for you, and I know it. We're friends. I'll do anything for my friends."

She nodded, then looked back at her babies. I snuck out while she was involved in listening to their childish babble and walked back to the house. With the griffins pushed further down the timeline, we could concentrate on the vampires.

I was exhausted by the time I'd landed back at the house. The stress and the magic use had drained me some-what, so I was grateful to see Gabe and Mr. Mittens in the kitchen when I walked in.

Gabe took one look at my face and said with a smile, "It worked out."

I don't know how he read me so well, because I'm sure I was a dirty, tousled mess with permanent frown lines at the moment.

"Yes, we've come to a truce that will allow Brightfeather to raise her chicks as she wishes, while making their grand-parents happy. And my grandfather will help me do my part to seal the deal."

"That's great news." He picked me up and swung me around, giving me a sound kiss.

Mr. Mittens jumped up on the table. I noticed, and so he didn't make me pay later, I added, "I couldn't have done it without the intimidation factor from Mr. Mittens, or Goch and Megan's lift to the Griffin Aerie. They were integral."

Gabe leaned over and gave Mr. Mittens a scratch behind his ears.

Well, I didn't do much, but I am ready for my supper, Mr. Mittens said smugly, reminding me the day was growing late.

"Did you see anything of the gargoyle festivities?" I asked Gabe, feeling like I'd abandoned my guests, although I knew that Madison had everything well in hand.

"Some, they're having a grand time, don't worry." He reached up and gently smoothed the skin between my eyebrows that must have been pinched together with worry. I smiled and leaned into him.

"You know me well," I said.

He held me tight for a moment, then released me to make my cat's meal. I bustled around and presented it to him with cream on the side.

As I watched him tuck in, I thought I'd tease him a bit. "You know, on earth, we don't give cats cream; it's not good for them."

He growled and lapped up some cream. Those *weak creatures can hardly be called cats.*

I laughed. "Yes, I'm sure. Luckily, you are much tougher."

Hmpf.

We left him to his meal and wandered into the bedroom. I needed to get cleaned up, see what I could do to help Madison, and check if any of the gargoyles staying needed anything. Megan had been back longer, so I was sure she'd already done that, but I had to check. Also, I needed to see Sorcha and crew and have them release the griffin spy.

Once I was done with those tasks, Gabe and I arrived outside in time to see the gargoyle flying games begin. Since that involved copious amounts of alcohol equivalent to some frat house drinking game, the festivities were either going to end with an injury or property damage. After the third drunken gargoyle ripped the top off my favorite Douglas Fir, I called the games done and sent everyone to bed to sleep it off.

Sam gave me a strange look as he also went inside, and I wondered if I'd stepped on his toes. He was also blitzed, so I figured we'd talk in the morning, if he remembered. Once the gargoyles were in their rooms, I finally allowed myself to go gratefully to bed.

Chapter Thirty-Four

I expected to sleep like the dead, as exhausted as I had been, but too many worries wore me down, and I slept fitfully. I finally gave up and got up around five in the morning. Since Gabe's alarm would sound in thirty more minutes, I snuck out and went into my office so I wouldn't disturb him.

I wanted to come up with a real plan, not just a knee-jerk reaction like I'd been doing up until now. The problem? I was no general. I wasn't even good at chess. No matter how I laid out everything I knew, I couldn't organize an offensive, past "go there, fight, win, and leave."

I must have been really tired. Somehow in the anxiety and flurry of activity with the griffins, I'd forgotten for a moment that some of history's greatest generals were sleeping it off under my roof.

I slapped myself on the forehead. "Idiot."

I needed to give Sam all the information and let him come up with a plan. Once that thought crystallized, I relaxed. I heard Gabe's alarm and hurried back to the bedroom. He was sitting on the edge of the bed, scrubbing sleep out of his eyes. I threw myself at him and sat on his lap, my legs wrapped around his waist and my arms around his neck.

"I'm going to let Alexander the Great and Genghis Kahn get us out of the vampire business. Whaddya think?" I murmured into his neck.

He laughed and wrapped his arms tightly around my waist. "I think it's about time you let the experts do this, so we can sit back with a mojito and watch."

I leaned back from him, looking into his hazel eyes, which were currently bright green against the blood shot whites.

"I'm usually being attacked, and I don't have time to come up with a plan." I sulked. Although I knew he was teasing me.

He pulled me in tight again, and I pressed my nose to the joining of his neck and shoulder and breathed him in. His scent was a comfort—soap, sleep sweat, and under it, him. I clung to him long enough he had to disentangle me.

"I have to go to work, and if you stay in this position, it will be awkward when I try to get dressed," he teased, but I could hear the reluctance to let me go.

I laughed and flopped onto the bed. I wanted to wait for him to get out of the bathroom and watch him dress, but my adventures the day before and lack of sleep meant I crashed hard when he was in the shower. I think I remembered him leaning down to kiss me before he left.

The pounding on my bedroom door was what awakened me for the day.

"Brigid, get out here." Megan's voice sounded a little

desperate. I looked at my phone. It was almost eleven. I groaned and threw on my clothes.

"What's going on?" I asked when I finally emerged.

She grabbed my hand and started to tug me towards the back. There was a tinge of panic in her voice. "It's Merlin and the griffins."

"Griffins? They aren't supposed to be here until after noon."

"It's not the royals, it's the guard for the chicks. Just come on."

I was still slow, barely awake, and I hadn't had my coffee. I let her drag me out the back.

Sure enough, the enchanter was standing toe to toe, figuratively, with a hulking griffin guard. This guy was the largest griffin I'd seen to date. He was tawny colored on his lion half, and his eagle half appeared to be a large golden eagle with towering ear tufts that added to his height and intimidation factor. His body being covered with scars also added to that, as did the segmented armor he wore over his vulnerable neck and chest areas.

"What's going on?" I asked in my firmest tone.

Neither of them looked at me or answered. I gathered up my air magic and shoved both of them away from each other. Then I stood between them. I raised my voice as loud as I could without screaming. "What. Is. Going. On?!"

Finally, both of them looked at me. I looked at the griffin. "I assume you are here to protect the royal chicks?"

He gave a stiff nod. Probably more from the armor, then from anything else.

"I suggest you go check on them then," I said dismissively. "If you require an escort, I can take you in a few moments."

The griffin gave a stiff little bow.

I whirled on Merlin. "What are you doing here?"

He chuckled and the suave, charming Merlin appeared. "I'm checking in with my new allies."

I squinted at him, trying to figure his angle. "Why?"

He looked at the ground, then back up at me. "I might have some intel that is useful."

"Oh, you might? Then why are you fighting with a griffin?"

He waved away my question like it wasn't important. "That was personal. I hadn't expected to find my old friend here, and we have a small score to settle."

"Friend?" I didn't settle scores with my friends, and my voice reflected my incredulity.

He shrugged. "A euphemism."

"He owes you money?"

"Something like that." But he didn't elaborate.

"Hmmm."

I let it go. It didn't seem to have a bearing on our current problems. "What's your news?"

"I think it'd be better to share with your gargoyle buddies, if they're still around."

"They are. Megan will get them. I'm going to take 'your friend' to Brightfeather, and I'll meet you back here."

He tucked his hands in his pockets. "Sounds good." He looked at Megan who'd been watching quietly. "Lead on MacDuff."

"Hmpf," Megan said, and I laughed a bit at her perfect Mr. Mittens impression. But she had him follow her into the house.

"This will require me to touch you," I informed the griffin. He gave a short nod, and I placed my hand on his side. We walked to Brightfeather. I couldn't remember if I'd told her about the mandatory guard, so it took a moment to introduce them, and I reminded her that the in-laws would be coming around soon.

She took it graciously, and I walked back, directly into my kitchen. No one was there, so I went to the dining room to find all the gargoyles, Megan, Mr. Mittens, and Merlin, waiting for me.

Chapter Thirty-Five

"So, what's the intel?" I asked before I even sat down. Curiosity and mistrust warring inside of me.

Merlin chuckled. "Right to the point and with such a lovely lunch spread." He waved his hands at the laden buffet.

"You're welcome to stay and eat after," I said with a sniff.

"Fine, I took the liberty of visiting the vampires directly to check out the lay of the land, so to speak." He kept up with the shit-eating grin.

I narrowed my eyes at him. "And how did you do that exactly?" Great, I should have been less trusting and more suspicious. He probably walked in with a big old invitation from Vic. He was working with them. I felt sick.

"Why magic, of course." He made a dramatic movement with his hands. I felt the Fae magic build, and he disappeared from sight. Shadow magic.

I felt a little relief. Maybe he wasn't working with the vamps after all.

He reappeared three seconds later. His grin was still plastered on his face, like that was impressive. We knew who he was. The demo wasn't necessary. In fact, it felt a little braggy.

"And?" I said, ignoring his demonstration.

That wiped the grin from his face and knocked the wind out of his sails. He leaned forward, elbows on his knees. "And I know how we'll get in."

Well, that would be good news. If we could trust him. I wondered why he was pushing my buttons. I hadn't been suspicious of Sofia or Scott. Of course, I was newly out of an abusive relationship, and I had no real people skills. Maybe I'd gone too far the other way? Maybe it was his complete and utter confidence or bravado. I wasn't sure. I did know that I shouldn't trust my instincts, they hadn't been right yet.

I sighed. "OK, that's good news. I was going to ask Sam here if he'd help plan the offensive. I'm no general, but he was, as was George."

Sam blinked, surprise written all over his face, and smiled. "I'd be delighted."

I looked at George, who grunted in the affirmative.

"OK, let's eat and talk."

We did. When lunch was over, I was satisfied that we had a decent plan. I also felt, under the anxiety and fear, that maybe, just maybe, we could win.

We'd just finished or at least my part was finished, when the griffins arrived for their first visitation. Since they needed to check in with me and give me a copy of the agreement, Mr. Mittens and I stood in the parking lot about thirty seconds before they arrived. The king and queen and five attendants landed gracefully in a cloud of feathers.

I held my hair back until all had settled around us and let it drop. We walked out to greet the royals.

I gave a short court bow, one you'd give to an equal, and waited.

We have the agreement, the king said and gestured to an attendant. The tawny colored griffin had a satchel slung over its neck. It reached inside and produced a scroll. I unwrapped the leather cover and unrolled it. Sure enough, it had been translated into English, and all the points I remembered were there with a royal sigil signing it at the bottom. I nodded and rerolled it.

Mr. Mittens stood at attention in his full Splintercat glory, coiled and ready to spring at anyone that moved or looked funny. I placed a hand on his shoulder and said, "all is well."

I felt a tiny twitch of muscle, but he didn't relent in his ready state.

"Please wait here, and I'll go and retrieve your family."

The queen gave a terse nod. If she'd been human, I'm sure her lips would be in a taut judgmental line. I took a step and walked to the nest.

Brightfeather was ready. She'd groomed, which was something she'd been slack on. The stress had left her disheveled and unkempt, but now, she looked the part of the proud princess. The chicks were also groomed, as well as chicks with a combination of baby fluff and new feathers could look. They appeared serious, so I knew they'd had a stern talking to. It didn't stop my little namesake from bouncing around and bumping against my legs. I bent over and smoothed her feathers back into place.

Aunty Brigid! Her tiny voice echoed in my mind. I looked at Brightfeather, tears thick in my throat.

"They are speaking now?" I managed to choke out over the lump in my throat.

Brightfeather's eyes sparkled with pride. *They are very bright. A power boost from Faerie didn't hurt either.*

I gave little Brigid a pat on her owl head and looked into her eyes. "Oh, my precious one!"

That was the cue for the others to crowd me, saying in their high-pitched mental voices the few words they knew. I laughed and patted all of them. "You are so terribly bright! Your grandparents will be amazed at you."

That brought a tremble to the little body still pressed against my leg.

I don't want to leave here, aunty.

"Oh, baby, you don't have to. They will come here to visit you or at my nest, anyway. We are only going a few acres away. Like when we visited Uncle Lugh in Faerie, only not as far."

Will you be there? Her large, round owl eyes were luminous when she looked at me—full of love and trust. I patted her on the head again. "Of course, my love."

"Now, gather round just like before, and I'll walk you all to the house. Ready?" I scooped up little Brigid, and the boys clung to my legs. I freed a hand from the solid warm body of the chick and pressed it against Brightfeather, and we walked.

Chapter Thirty-Six

We appeared in the spot I'd recently vacated. Brightfeather shook out her feathers and checked on her children. They were fine, although they continued to cling to my legs and little Brigid had tucked her head under my armpit.

I stroked her downy feathers and down over her baby fur. "It's OK," I whispered.

Brightfeather strode forward and bowed low to her in-laws. *I present my children,* she said in griffin, which sounded a bit like listening to eagles—all high-pitched whistles. But she let her mental voice translate into my head. *My first born, Umber, named for his father.*

Umber, little darling that he was, put on a brave stance and walked forward when he was announced. He gave a clumsy bow to his grandparents. I wanted to laugh at how cute it was, but I could feel his stress, and held it in. He was a serious fellow.

Brightstorm, my second son, named for my father. Little Brightstorm walked forward, trying to copy his brother. He stumbled once but made a better bow. He was the silly one, but he wished to be taken seriously.

I kissed Brigid on her head and set her down on the ground. She was still trembling, but being a brave little thing, she waited until her name was called and walked forward to give her bow.

Brigid, my daughter, third born, and named for my Fae friend, Brightfeather announced.

I watched the grandparents look over their grandchildren. They were transfixed by little Brigid. I knew she looked startlingly similar to Umber, their father, and I was expecting them to be affected at seeing her.

She is so like... the queen began but trailed off. It was obvious what she meant.

One thing they couldn't do was doubt whose child she was. If that had been part of their issue with Brightfeather keeping the children from them, the sight of little Brigid allayed that quickly.

After her emotional reaction, the queen straightened up and gave an imperious snort. *You have broken convention by naming them before they were presented to court,* she said to Brightfeather with a sneer.

I wished I could get away with slapping her, but I'd be dead before my hand came forward, so I clenched my teeth and balled my fists instead. She was so stubborn. Why couldn't she just forgive and forget? This was all that was left of her *family.*

Brightfeather was a little better at this game, though. I should have known she'd know what to do. She understood it was grief that pushed the royals to be so cruel.

I apologize, my queen. I was lost in my grief and didn't know what to do. I named them before I thought about the consequences. Please forgive me. She ducked into another low bow.

That was a proper suck-up if I'd ever seen one. I raised a hand to cover my grin.

The king took charge. His gaze had been transfixed on the griffinettes. He was ready—more ready than the queen—to get the reunion going.

The names are adequate, we will accept them.

He gestured to the griffin that had given me the scroll. He took out a wax tablet from his satchel and recorded what I assumed were the children's names onto it. Once the scribe finished, the king declared that the names were now official.

Brightfeather beamed.

The king and queen approached the chicks which were now huddled together, looking up at all the scary new griffins surrounding them. They looked so tiny next to the adults. Mr. Mittens stalked closer to them, and they unconsciously huddled close to his legs.

We won't harm our grandchildren, the king intoned with force. I flinched from the anger in his tone, but Mr. Mittens didn't move.

Nothing will harm them while I am here, Mr. Mittens said, his eyes flinty.

I was pretty sure he could take two or three full-grown griffins, but not all of them. My hands began to sweat, I gathered my power and held lightning in my mind. My hair floated with static. If Mr. Mittens lost control and attacked, the griffins would slaughter us. I couldn't react. And I couldn't let him either. No matter what. I let the magic go.

I put a hand on his side. "They will be fine," I whispered. "Let their grandparents see them."

Hmpf. He reached down and licked each baby griffin's head, then took a step back.

"As you can see, they are well-protected here," I said,

trying to save the moment without creating a political incident.

Yes, the king said. *I see.*

The king and queen bent down and examined the chicks, a sound like a purr rumbling forth from them. I startled—more used to hearing eagle noises from the griffins than cat ones—but the sound was soothing, and the chicks responded. It was slow, but they had the trusting natures of the young and loved. Soon, they were their normal selves, playing and wrestling at the feet of their grandparents, who looked on indulgently.

Our son produced fine children, the king said to his mate, although he let us all hear. He was proud, and I finally relaxed.

They stayed an hour, perhaps, and by the time they were ready to leave, the king had allowed the chicks to climb on him, and they'd all wrestled around. It was precious to see. Particularly, because Brightfeather and the queen stood together, both watching with love in their eyes. I knew the family was on its way to healing.

Now, we just needed to defeat the vampires, return the collar and the other item Merlin was making for the dragons, and this nightmare would be over. No more war. I'd be able to run my inn without fear for my guests. It was so near. My heart's desire stood a touch out of reach of my fingertips, and all I had to do was stretch a tiny bit to grasp it.

Chapter Thirty-Seven

The vampires had been quiet. Too quiet. They'd let us plot and scheme and prepare for our offensive.

The gargoyle's left, their reunion over, but they were planning to come back in a few days when we set our new, brilliant plan in motion.

I was a fool. I'd waited too long.

The griffins left after their visit, satisfied and content—their visitation schedule arranged, all family members satisfied, and the future of the kingdom solidly in hand. Brightfeather had also agreed to one more guard, so I felt better about their safety in my dangerous woods.

The baincapall hadn't liked the griffins descending on us, but I gave them a copy of the schedule so they wouldn't challenge any visiting griffins. No sense creating an inter-realm issue, right?

With all of that completed, and with an intense feeling of satisfaction, I planned to sit curled up on the couch in my drawing room with Gabe and watch TV—something we hadn't done in ages. We had the popcorn ready, a fire blazing in the hearth, and a fuzzy blanket to snuggle up in —nothing but uninterrupted pleasure planned.

And that's when the vampires attacked. Bastards.

Vic had done it. He'd lulled me into a false sense of security, of thinking I had the upper hand. That crap with his wife? I'd believed him. I'd fallen for the grateful husband routine and believed he'd generously give us breathing room. While the truth was, he'd just been waiting for the gargoyles to leave to end me and mine once and for all.

I didn't even have the shield up on the house. I'd taken it down to preserve it for another day. I almost laughed. I was going to use it to protect the house when we went on the offensive.

Like I said, I was an utter fool.

We'd just settled on the couch when the explosive force of every window blowing in hit us. Glass sparkled in the air, and I threw up my air magic to protect us. I was a moment late, and splinters of glass cut us both. Once my air shield was up, Gabe healed me and himself, and we rushed from the room.

Megan and Luke came pounding down the stairs. Megan was unharmed, but there were streaks of blood on her skin and clothing; I was sure I looked the same. She'd been constantly wearing her sheath in a magic ball, and even in that form, it had healed her. Luke had shifted into his wolf, so whatever hurt he'd received from the glass had been healed already.

It was us, Mr. Mittens, our eight baincapall guards, and maybe Jim and Chef Jack against who knew how many ancient and new vampires. We gathered in the foyer.

"Where are the bats?" Megan asked, eyes wide. She held her sword and shield in her hands. Luke pressed to her side.

"I don't know." I looked around, whirling quickly to make sure nobody had surrounded us in the house.

Mr. Mittens had rushed in at the same time as Megan and Luke—he'd been asleep on the bed. His fur was mussed, and he had his grumpiest face on.

"They must have blown the windows out with… magic." Panic was building in my heart. They hadn't used much magic against me. Did Merlin betray us? I didn't know if I could stand against him if he had. He was a famous enchanter with Fae magic, and he'd been using his magic, fully trained, for centuries. I reached out with my senses.

Weary relief filled me as a new reality set in. This wasn't Fae magic. They must have gathered the remnants of the coven together, or they'd brought in more witches when they brought in extra vampires. Still, it looked as though Merlin hadn't betrayed us.

That meant he might still be willing to help if we could contact him. I pulled out my phone, and another pulse of magic hit the house.

I handed the phone to Gabe. "I've got to get the shield up, please text Grandfather, Dana, and Merlin, Jim, Jack, the werewolves, the gargoyles, and Sorcha and tell them we are under attack and need help." It was a poor plan. I doubted the werewolves or the gargoyles would make it before the vamps had utterly destroyed us. I hoped those closer to us and the realm walkers could get to us in time. For once, I hoped my grandfather and Dana were near their phones.

Gabe nodded once, already buried in my phone contacts. I rushed to the bedroom and threw open my top dresser door. I put every magic ball I had in my pockets and grabbed the bag of explosive fireballs as well.

"Come out, come out, wherever you are!" Bella's voice sing-songed out to us.

I knew they could enter the house. They'd done it before. Bella had been invited in freely once, and either the whole "vampires had to be invited in" thing was propaganda, or we'd just blown it the first time she'd come to the door to deliver a letter. She'd used her invite to let the rest of the vampiric world into my house. Maybe resetting her vampireness would reset the invite? Probably not. Too many vampires had been through here. That little protection was long gone.

So why had they blown all the windows and stayed outside?

The shield was down... Ah, but maybe they didn't know that. They'd witnessed what had happened at the last battle, as several of their compatriots had flashed into ash when they came into contact with it. Maybe that knowledge was holding them back. If so, it wouldn't be long until a master vamp used an underling as cannon fodder. We probably only had seconds.

"Any ideas?" I asked.

I handed the bag of fireballs to Gabe. He was the only one that could use them currently. Megan's hands were full, Luke was in wolf form, and I already had fire at my beck and call.

"We go out and fight!" Megan said.

"Yeah, I don't see another choice either. But we don't have to go out the doors where they're expecting it." I finally got my brain working. "Megan and Luke, go out the side window by the rose garden. Mr. Mittens, you take the roof; Gabe and I will go out the bedroom window. Let's get free and see if we can flank them."

We set off. Mr. Mittens was up the stairs before I could

even finish talking. With his ability to jump and his keen cat eyes, the roof was the perfect place for him. I put out a mental call to Goch, but he was either off planet, or he didn't reply to me. I also called Brightfeather but told her to stay away. I doubted the vamps could find her or would go after her as long as she didn't join us. She wasn't on their radar.

I did wish we had her fighting skills though.

Luke and Megan had slunk to the far side of the house to access the window past the laundry room. Gabe and I entered our bedroom and approached the picture window in the turret area with trepidation.

The night outside was black as pitch. No moon. The witches must be strong to blow out the windows without the help of moon magic. We crouched and peeked through the empty frame. Our feet had crunched on glass, so we'd lost the element of stealth. I just hoped that the vamps were at the two doors and not watching the windows.

I couldn't see anyone, and from Gabe's head shake, he hadn't either. I eased myself onto the windowsill and swung my legs over.

That was the moment the vamps sent in their cannon fodder.

Chapter Thirty-Eight

I heard a "No shield!" shout go up, and I jumped down. Gabe landing next to me a second later. We'd have to run over the driveway to reach cover, but we'd be exposed.

I wished I had my cat's eyes right now. But I had one better. "Close your eyes, this is gonna hurt," I whispered to Gabe. He squeezed my arm, and I knew he'd done it. I built up all the light magic I could hold and shot it out in a pulse. Vamps screamed in agony as their eyes burned with the intense light. My crazy extra magic had flared it a bit brighter, and I'm sure a few young vamps were ashed.

While they screamed, momentarily blinded, I threw the shield ball and activated it. At least the house would be safe now, and if any vamps were inside, they wouldn't be getting out anytime soon.

That only took a moment. We ran across the drive and slunk into the trees. It was so dark, that although I knew my land, we stumbled and fell our way around the parking lot, so we were behind the vamps facing my back door.

We crouched next to a tree. Although the magic pulse

that had broken my windows had also destroyed the house's exterior lights, the lone streetlamp that lent a warm glow to the parking area was unaffected. It wasn't a strong light, only bright enough that guests wouldn't stumble before they reached the bright house floods, but it was enough that I could see my worst nightmare.

Eleven man-sized bats stood staring at the house, surrounded by a dozen or more cloaked witches.

That meant each of those man bats were ancient master vamps. Equal to or stronger than Vic. A chill ran down my spine. Unless backup came soon, we were going to die. The vamps had outsmarted me good. We should have attacked when we thought they still hadn't brought over help. If only I hadn't been distracted by all the side quests.

I studied the man-sized bat vampires. Which one was Vic? It was impossible to tell, but it had to be one of the three middle vamps since this was his show, and ego was his middle name. I pulled up my power and shot a lightning bolt at them. I would probably only get one chance with these old vamps, so I poured everything into that one bolt.

Lightning is fickle. I could aim it generally, but it still had a mind of its own. The vamp I'd aimed at was perfectly safe, but the one next to it took the full brunt. A brief cry, and a puff of ash later and I'd narrowed down the pack to ten—too bad they hadn't been wearing metal armor. However, it showed the rest where I was. They burst into flight like a startled flock of ravens, each going a separate direction from the others. Our small advantage flew away.

I knew it was a onetime freebie, and I didn't regret taking it—one less master vamp to deal with. But we had to move from our hiding place.

The young vamps, it looked like thousands to my affected sight, flew in every direction as well. Gabe started chucking explosive fireballs at any that clustered together, and I began to throw fire as well. Even with that, the sheer numbers were going to crush us soon without help.

I threw everything I had at them. Fire, water, light, lightning, and although dozens fell, more took their place.

We were surrounded. The weight of their numbers pressed on us, and Gabe and I stood back-to-back. He flung fireballs, and I flung magic, and still there were more vamps. This was it. Worse than facing my own death was knowing that I'd caused Gabe's. I reached back and grasped his hand. He was out of fireballs, and the sack hung loosely in the hand I grasped.

"I love you," I said.

"I love you, too."

I wanted to realm walk us away, but I couldn't leave Luke and Megan. *The roof*, I thought. It should be safe—Mr. Mittens was there. I took firm hold of Gabe's hand and walked.

The roof wasn't empty. I parked us right in the grasp of a master vamp. His hand grasped my throat.

I shut my eyes, waiting for cold teeth to rip out my throat. When it didn't happen, I opened them again, and stared into his icy gaze. It wasn't Vic; I'd never met this creature.

Where Vic was handsome, this thing was twisted and ugly, reflecting the monster within.

It had lank dark hair, blazing red eyes, and a sneer that showed its sharp teeth.

"So, you are the bit that has confounded the great Ludovic," it said with a growling rasp over a thick accent. It threw back its head and laughed.

Gabe reached out a hand to devamp it, I supposed. But his hand stopped before he could touch the creature.

"Be gone, human!" the vamp roared. Gabe turned and stumbled towards the edge of the roof, caught in the vamp's compulsion.

"I can feel the magic in your blood." It licked its blood-red lips with a pointed tongue.

Then it moved so fast, I didn't see it, and its hand grasping my throat yanked me against its chest. The air whooshed out of my lungs, and my neck ached. I knew if I survived, I'd suffer whiplash symptoms for weeks if Gabe wasn't around to heal me.

I reached for my magic as its fangs came at me, and I panicked. There was nothing there. No magic. I was certain my death was now.

A dark cloud of fur and fangs descended, and I was suddenly free, the hand whipping away from my throat. The sudden release sent me reeling backward into Gabe who had stopped a few feet behind me as he fought against the compulsion. We rolled towards the edge.

Mr. Mittens ripped the vamp with teeth and claws until it burst into ash.

Use your magic, pet, he said before bounding off to rip apart more vamps.

I blinked, and the panic and the hold the master had on me vanished. I realized it had bespelled me, mesmerized me. Damn those creepy bastards. Anger took hold of me as I grabbed ahold of my magic and blasted away.

Down to nine masters, and a zillion other vamps, plus the witches. Would I never be free of them?

I heard a truck racing up my drive. I sure hoped that it was the Whelans and not some innocent humans. It roared around the house and rammed into three witches and several vamps. Werewolves poured over the sides of the truck, and the tide momentarily turned.

Noah was the driver. As alpha, he could turn faster than the others. He opened the door and was in his wolf skin before I could have exited a vehicle. Five wolves had joined us. I didn't know who they were, past Noah's black wolf, but I figured it was the rest of the Whelans.

Luke raced to join his family, and I searched for Megan. She was fighting close to the woods with the giant baincapall warriors.

Just as I was about to look away, an immense tiger leaped from the woods onto a master vamp. Chef Jack had joined the fray. My breath caught. We were down to eight masters now. I felt hope well in my heart. We had a chance now. I didn't have time to search for Jim, but he'd be above us, hopefully going through vampire bats like candy. Thank heavens. Too bad Milk Dud was still a foal, this is the one time I wished we had an adult unicorn around to kick ass.

My hope was short-lived. Even with the extra help, we were still losing. They were pushing us together, surrounding us, attempting to trap us. The magic continued to flow around me, but I knew it was only a matter of time before my reserves were empty, and I wouldn't be able to draw enough from the link because I was burning through it too fast. The collar around my neck was fully charged, but if we didn't get this wrapped up soon, I'd burn through it as well.

We needed reinforcements. We needed to get behind the shield I'd placed around the house. We needed to end this for good.

Chapter Thirty-Nine

We couldn't reach the house. They'd done it—surrounded us, and with overwhelming numbers they drove us together into a tight knot.

The fighting stopped. Vic came forward, gloating.

"Drop the shield on the house," he commanded, and I felt the power of the master vamp push down on me.

My resistance waned. I managed to force out one plaintive, "Why?"

I had no idea why they wanted in the house. We were out here. What did he think he'd find inside?

He smiled a fang filled nightmare. "I've figured out your secret."

I felt confused, but even that was far away as his power beat down on my meager defenses. "What secret?" I croaked out.

"Don't be coy. I know you are Fae."

That wasn't a secret; his wife's sister had known that and tried to exploit it by killing me and stealing my magic.

"So?"

His eyes grew red, and he hissed. "You have a link to Faerie hiding in that house, and I will have it!"

I blinked at his fury, his breath reeked of old blood and death, and I stepped back, bumping into Gabe.

Boy was he ever wrong. Not about the link but about the location. I tried to keep my face blank. "Why do you think that?" I asked coyly, the jolt from running into Gabe helping me break free of the master's control for a moment.

Gabe's hands pressed on my back, and I could feel the warmth of his magic. It helped me free myself from the compulsion even more.

Vic frowned as I continued to defy him. He stepped closer. Using the sharpened nail on his finger, he pierced the skin under my chin, hooking it on the bone, and drew me close.

I flinched at the pain, terror gripping my heart in an icy hold. He pulled me from Gabe's reach, and my mind clouded again.

The blood trickled down my skin, and Vic inhaled, and then his cold tongue licked my throat clean. I shuddered with revulsion.

"It's hidden in your attic."

I almost laughed but held it in. He mustn't have licked enough of my blood to know the truth. He didn't know about the waterfall. Sure, there was a focus in my attic, but the link wasn't there. But if that was what he thought, I had to use it somehow to my advantage.

"You'll never get in there. Even if you could, the attic is protected."

It was. Someone of my blood had to be within three feet of it to even see the door.

I looked around, trying to see a way out of this. I didn't

see Mr. Mittens anywhere. A tiny part of me relaxed. He was free. He'd find a way to rescue us. I knew it.

"Remove the shield."

"No."

The warmth at my back was ripped away. A master vamp pulled Gabe around to stand behind Vic.

"Remove it or I remove his head and lap his blood as it spurts from the stump of his neck."

My knees went weak. I looked at Gabe's face. He was serene.

"Don't do it," he whispered, and the vamp that held him yanked his head back by the hair, baring his throat.

Gabe laughed, and the master vamp screamed. Gabe had a hand on the vamp's wrist and was healing him.

I laughed. That's when Bella stepped forward and hit Gabe with her taser. He crumpled.

The master he'd started to heal coughed, but he straightened. The pink coming into his cheeks faded, and he turned his gaze to Gabe, fury burning like coals in his eyes.

"Don't hurt him," I whispered. "I'll do it." I had to say something, the master who had Gabe wasn't going to stop without a distraction.

Vic smiled. "Of course you will."

I could delay this, take time dropping the shield, stall going to the attic, but he'd get us there eventually, and as soon as I did, we were all good as dead. Would dragging my feet help us? Was anyone else coming?

I glanced around for any help, but the vamps had us.

A warm pulse of realm walking magic struck me, and I continued to scan around me, but Vic yanked my arm and pulled me up to the house.

"Any time now," he said, almost friendly.

I swallowed. Slowly, I raised my arms, delaying, taking

as much time as I could. Did the magic pulse mean someone had arrived to help? Was it my cat getting into a better position?

A sharp nail poked into my side, and I flinched.

"Now, Brigid."

I nodded and said the words of release. The shield fell.

"Now, that wasn't so hard, was it?" Vic said.

I didn't say anything.

Vic yanked my arm, pulling me to the house, and dragged me stumbling up the porch stairs. We were only three stories away from the truth, and it was rushing towards me with a brutal finality.

Several witches followed. One's hood had fallen away, and I recognized Vic's wife. She grinned at me. "We'll get your magic now, Fae bitch."

I lunged at her, and my nails raked a momentary bright mark down her face as I clawed her. Her vamp healing closed them instantly, but I'd made her bleed.

She lunged back towards me, her fangs bared. Vic stopped her. "You can have her after, love."

She hissed but retreated a step.

Vic continued to yank me along with him. We were through the kitchen. A sob tore through my guts, and tears streaked down my cheeks like burning brands. Death I could face, but watching Gabe die? Megan? I didn't think I could do it.

Vic pulled on my arm so hard, a popping noise filled my ears as my shoulder was wrenched out of joint. A burning pain seared through me and burst from my throat in a scream.

Vic released my arm, and I stumbled forward. I grasped my arm with my other hand.

Gabe shouted. I looked at him, my eyes unfocused.

"Let me heal her," he yelled.

"Heal them," I said, a sudden inexplicable laugh bubbling up. He hadn't made any vamps human that I'd noticed…yet. Although, he'd tried.

Vic snarled. "You heal anyone, and I'll drain her in front of you."

I wanted to hit him with a bolt of lightning, but the pain made it so I couldn't hold the magic in my mind firmly. All I managed was a little static.

Gabe stood up straight. "Let me heal her. She's no good to you broken or dead."

In answer, Vic opened his mouth, unhinging his jaw, and leaned over me. He pulled back at the last moment and smiled at Gabe. "No."

Then he grabbed my wounded arm and continued to pull on me. My vision turned black around the edges, and nausea clawed up my guts. My vision narrowed to a tunnel and the next thing I knew I was looking at the ceiling, my back pressed against the stairs.

"Heal her, this is too much of a delay," Vic growled. I guess he'd overestimated my ability to bear pain.

Gabe bent over me, his hands pressed to my abused shoulder, and the warmth of his magic poured into me. There was a snick as the shoulder reattached in its proper place; the pain of that almost sent me back into a faint. But then the warmth filled me, and the pain receded to nothing. I breathed a sigh of relief and smiled at my love.

He was yanked back. He whirled on the vamp that had him and placed his hands firmly on it. This one wasn't a master, and in seconds, it went from the greyish tone of the vamps to pink and human, and then it rotted alive and finally, turned to ash.

Bella hit Gabe with her taser, and he fell back, landing on the myrtlewood floor in a daze.

I grasped hold of my magic and sent a gust of wind to knock her off her feet, and I aimed a blast of lightning at Vic at the same time. Bella flew over the banister, but Vic sidestepped me and a young vamp burst into ash. Vic turned his gaze on me and all the weight of compulsion he had pressed down on me.

"Get up," Vic commanded. I turned and scampered to my feet, swaying a moment as the blood rushed from my head, before steadying.

He yanked on my arm but was more careful not to pull it out of its socket again. Having to let Gabe heal me, and the both of us killing his underlings must have embarrassed him in front of his wife and creepy colleagues.

Soon enough, we stepped onto the third-floor landing. As we approached, the smooth wall was all they could see. However, once I was close enough, the door appeared. Vic smiled down on me.

"Open it."

"It's just a door; anyone can open it." My small defiance enraged him, and he flung me at the door. I hit it and slid down, stunned. But his snarling face and strong compulsion encouraged me to stand and fling open the door quickly.

I rushed inside, turning on the lights.

The comforting space, full of my family's history, failed to do its job of putting me at ease. There were a few more stairs to climb, and soon enough, the group was gathered at the top in my attic.

Chapter Forty

Vic looked around. Even if the link was here, which it wasn't, you couldn't see it. I'd gazed around the waterfall forever, looking, but the link wasn't visible. It was a rent in the space-time continuum—at least that's how I thought about it. I really had no idea what it was or how it worked. Although, I'd have to figure that out soon to balance my debt with the griffins—if I lived. I felt another one of those senseless hysterical giggles rise up and choked it down.

"Where is it?" Vic demanded.

I shrugged. "I don't know how to tell you to find it, it isn't a thing."

Apparently, my ability to fight his compulsion, no matter how small of a pushback it was, enraged him. He backhanded me. The crack of his hand hitting my face knocked me senseless, and I flew into a pile of boxes. I lay there, trying to come back to grips with reality. He commanded the witches to search for the link. At least he was waiting to find it before he killed us.

I struggled to my feet. Gabe watched, but a new vamp

stood beside him with a taser, careful not to let Gabe touch him. I noticed no one was holding him now, but he was as restrained by that taser as I was by the blow that had stunned me. I reached up to feel my face. It had already begun to swell. I had healing balls in my pockets, but it seemed foolish to burn one that could bring someone back from the brink of death on one swollen face.

I let the throb of pain keep me centered, letting it wash away the power of the master vamp.

"It's not here, my lord," a witch said.

The witch walked over by my favorite tulip-stained glass. For whatever reason, the windows in the attic were still intact. The magic here must have protected them.

The witch held out her arms and seemed to wiggle about. "There seems to be a concentration of Fae power, but it isn't the source," the witch continued.

I figured her quite brave to admit that since the master vamp didn't have a lot of self-control when he was angry.

Now that my head was clearing from the master's control, I needed to get close to Gabe so I could get us both out of this.

"Where is your power coming from?" The master roared.

"It comes from Faerie, you idiot," I answered, every bit of sarcasm I could put in my tone dripping from my tongue. I figured if I convinced him to hit me again, Gabe would have to heal me, or I'd be useless.

Once he touched me, we could realm walk away.

Of course, being hit on the same cheek was a lot less pleasant the second time, and I think I blacked out momentarily. However, it worked, because I woke up to the warmth of Gabe's magic. My eyes flicked to his; I grabbed his wrist and walked us out.

We arrived on the Fae practice planet in the same position. That was my first time walking without actually taking a step. Which was helpful to know was a possibility. Gabe pulled me to my feet.

"That was brilliant."

"Thanks, I would have done it sooner, but he kept me under pretty tight control," I apologized.

"How does your face feel?" He looked at me closely. "He broke your cheek and jawbone with that last blow."

"Much better, thank you."

"We need to go back. He still has everyone else. If we don't go, he'll kill them."

I nodded. "Time isn't a problem." I said it and realized it at the same time. We needed our allies. And now that I was thinking clearly, we could get them there in time.

He must have had the same thought at the same time because we both said, "Time," and then we laughed at each other in surprise.

Chef Jack, Jim, and the Whelans had come once we'd texted them, but my most powerful allies had not. But I had the gift of time. I just needed to get them there at the right moment.

"Well, how about that trip to Faerie?" I said to him.

"Sounds grand." He held out his elbow. I slipped my arm in his, and we walked.

I gave my grandfather the correct time to arrive with help and walked back to the gargoyle's reunion. I had gone to Faerie in the middle of their festivities, so I knew I wasn't around. It was almost impossible to share close space with yourself, so knowing I was gone made the trip easier.

I told Sam everything and swore him to secrecy. He had to go on as though he didn't know the information I was sharing, so we didn't screw up the timeline we'd already traveled. I told him when to arrive, and we walked back into chaos.

I set us down the moment we'd left, only back in the parking lot. Our friends were still being held by vampires, but they hadn't been harmed yet. They were waiting for Vic to locate my power source. Gabe and I were in the trees on the path to the waterfall, but on the other side of the simple barrier that kept careless beings from stumbling their way to the source.

It had worked on the vamps so far.

The lone streetlamp illuminated the scene well enough for us to see the parking lot, so we knew when Vic and his crew came streaming out of the house. He was heading straight for my friends. If I didn't show, he'd kill them. I felt that in my bones.

"I've got to go back out there," I said and pulled my arm from Gabe's. "Stay here."

I ran.

Vic saw me after I'd only taken two or three steps. He zipped to me at vamp speed. I didn't even have time to use my magic before he was on me. This time, he bent over and bit my neck. I cried out.

I remembered he could read everything I knew from my blood. He'd know where my power was now, and he had no reason to keep me alive. He was going to drain me.

I struggled weakly, trying to grasp a hold of my fire magic, but it was worthless. I was fully under the control of his power. I couldn't even raise a hand to push him back. I wondered why he hadn't done this sooner. Seemed easier…

I was fading. My thoughts were slow and far away. I watched the moonless sky.

A shadow made the night darker for an instant, and then a sound rent the air. Vic dropped me, and I lay on the ground, the cold seeping through me, pulling me down to the heart of the earth.

I felt a rough tongue lick my face, but I couldn't respond, or connect with what it was. My still body rocked as someone tried to move me. Then they were forcing something down my throat. I couldn't fight, and when they told me to swallow, I did. It took the last of my strength. I didn't even have enough left to blink. My eyes stared at the heavens.

The warmth started in my belly. Like an exploding star, it thrummed outward until I swear I could even feel it in the ends of my hair. I gasped, a single convulsion struck me, and my mind and body reconnected. I blinked.

Megan and Mr. Mittens stood over me.

"Can you walk?" Megan asked.

I moved my fingers and toes. Everything felt normal. I nodded, and she pulled me to a sitting position.

"What happened?" I asked.

"Merlin. Come on, we need to get back to the fight."

"He read my blood. He knows where the source of my power is," I said.

Megan frowned but kept looking towards the house and the battle. She shook her head. "We need to go."

"Gabe." I looked around. "Is he?"

"The vamps grabbed him, but I think he got loose, come on." She pulled me to my feet, and after a couple of stumbling steps, I ran after her and Mr. Mittens.

Chapter Forty-One

The gargoyles had arrived, as had my grandfather, Dana, and it looked like a dozen or so of my grandfather's warriors.

But the crowning ally, who I hadn't been able to contact, was Merlin. He was on the back of a massive red dragon, who was wearing a golden crown. I squinted. It couldn't be Goch? It wasn't. This dragon had two immense horns arching off his head and an unscarred face. It was…Darg? Goch's grandsire?

It had to be. I'd only seen him once, but it had to be him. I wondered how this had occurred.

My heart swelled. My friends had come through. I felt my legs wobble, and gratitude warmed me. The tide had turned.

Merlin and Darg swooped in and out of the light, the dragon's fire lighting up the night and burning bats to ash. Grandfather and his warriors were fighting the master vamps. Although the masters were down to seven, the fight seemed equally matched. The witches were chanting, and a red dome surrounded them. I looked at the master vamps. Yup, whatever the witches were doing, it had to be protecting those bastards. The gargoyles were ashing vamps everywhere I looked—land and sky. If I could stop the witches, this would be over—forever.

Even though Grandfather and his troops weren't as fast as the vamps, they had magic on their side—magic that was being blocked.

Mr. Mittens, who hadn't left my side, lunged and brought down a vamp that had snuck up on me. It turned to ash. His fur, usually tawny with spots in this form, was ash grey from all the vamps he'd killed. Only his glowing blue eyes were familiar.

"Mr. Mittens, we have to stop the witches."

Hmpf.

He bounded off and pounced at them but bounced off their ward.

"I'll try to disrupt the barrier, then you take care of them, OK?"

Yes.

I wasn't sure if I could break their spell from outside. When I'd been trapped by witches before, no one could get through. I'd had to disrupt things from the inside. But I was more powerful now and much better trained than I had been. I thought about weaving the strands of my elemental magic together, like I'd done to power up the collar. Would that get through?

I had to try.

First, I sent a lightning bolt, because it was a lot easier to do and might be enough.

It wasn't. It ricocheted away, frying several vampire bats as it went. It almost hit a gargoyle though, and I didn't want to do that.

I started to weave the elements together, gathering them in my mind. I could feel the wind of Mr. Mittens passage as he kept the vamps off me. I needed time to concentrate. Earth, water, fire, light, lightning, mind, spirit, aether, time, shadow, ice, reality, and air. Thirteen elements, the most of any Fae and one of only three known people to bear them in a thousand years. I could do this. Determined, I pulled raw power from the link and the collar, and with all the force I could draw, I unleashed the weave at the witches' red barrier.

The flash and accompanying blast blew everyone down. Vamps, wolves, and people rolled across my parking lot. I landed on my butt, which sent shockwaves up my spine and a shooting pain. I rolled to my side, groaning.

Finally, I pulled myself back up to see the witches. The blast had vaporized them and most of the vampires.

Mr. Mittens disappointed voice filled my mind. *You didn't save any witches for me.*

"Sorry, I think Vic's wife is still around. You're welcome to her."

Yes. A consolation prize.

I looked around. The seven master vamps were now being beaten back. I saw a lightning blast from my grandfather fry one. Fire from a warrior took out another. Then the rest fell quickly.

I cast about for Vic and his witch-vampire wife. I couldn't lose them. This wasn't over until they were dead. I also hadn't seen Bella since she went flying over the banister with her taser.

That wasn't good. He'd taken my blood. I could guess where he was heading next.

I raced up to my grandfather. My friends were slowly gathering back around him. Most of the vamps were gone, it was clean up only, and the gargoyles were finishing that job.

"Vic, Amber, and Bella are not here."

"They've probably been ashed," Megan said.

"No, they're missing, not dead. Something's wrong."

That had everyone else looking around.

"They've gone to the waterfall!" I shouted. "We can't let them access the link to Faerie."

I didn't know what Vic's endgame was, but something told me it involved my link and the witch that was his wife. What did they know that I didn't?

I started running. I didn't know who followed. I hadn't seen Gabe; we'd gotten separated. Mr. Mittens pulled ahead of me, so I knew I wasn't alone, and we hurried.

"Realm walk," I shouted to him, and then took my own advice. I stepped on the practice planet and barely paused before I was at the waterfall. Mr. Mittens arrived at nearly the same moment, and we both moved to my boulder. It was the closest you could physically get to the link. It floated somewhere above this boulder where I'd always been drawn, even as a small child. I scrambled up and stood atop it, Mr. Mittens poised in front of me.

We were alone. We'd gotten ahead of them. But we were also ahead of our backup. Stupid.

Chapter Forty-Two

For a second, I considered time walking and grabbing my friends to help, but there wasn't a lot of space up here. I also didn't know where the vamps were exactly. I scratched behind Mr. Mittens' ears. It was a different feeling than when he was in his Ragdoll form. Then his fur was like cottony silk. Now it was short and rough, the fur of a perfect apex predator. Mr. Mittens was worth ten of anyone else when it came to battle, anyway. I stood my ground.

I could hear the stamp of feet and the swish of clothing approaching. The last turn on the path that led here was tight, and you had to step up a bit, so we were out of the sight of the vampires for a moment while they were in ours.

I could feel Mr. Mittens' muscles bunch under my hand, and I gathered my magic. It was Vic, his wife Amber, Bella, and a handful of other vampires.

Vic was the largest threat, being a master vamp. I aimed my lightning bolt at him. Mr. Mittens leapt in front of me, and I pulled back. That gave the witch time to throw up a shield. Mr. Mittens bounced off hard.

He landed on his side and scrambled up quickly. Backing away to where there was more space for him to attack.

I cursed softly to myself; I'd been hoping for the element of surprise.

"So, this is the place of your power," Vic said, looking about.

I stayed quiet.

The witch held up her hands and moved them around as though she was searching. Then she pointed above my head. "There."

My heart sank. What were they going to do? Break my link? Take it somehow?

"What do you want?" I asked, my voice hard and cold.

Vic waved a hand. "It's simple, really. With this link, my witches can fill their wells whenever they wish."

"How? They can't access the power," I said uncertainly.

He shrugged and gestured for his wife to answer.

"A simple ritual will suffice," she answered with a sneer. "I would much prefer to take your Fae power, but that would only help me. The coven can fight over this."

So, the witches still wanted me dead, of course. All of this came down to the same old thing—they were jealous of my power. And since I was Fae, I was beneath them, so they should just take what they wanted.

I hoped backup was almost here. We needed a distraction so I could get around the witch's shield. I needed to keep them talking, delay them.

"You think it will be easy to kill me?" I asked. "You've been botching it for a while."

The witch's face reddened with her fury. "I haven't put my mind to it yet."

Mr. Mittens growled at her answer.

Megan and whoever she'd grabbed had to be close. They were right behind us, not far behind these fools.

I put a hand on Mr. Mittens. "Wait for my signal, and then go for Vic," I said silently.

The second my friends turned the corner; I would blast the vamps with everything I had. A distraction would hopefully give everyone on our side an advantage.

He will be ash.

I smiled to myself. Yes, he would be. All Mr. Mittens needed was an opening. I kept talking. "And you, *Master* bloodsucker…" I drawled out the master, dripping all the sarcasm I could call up on the word. "You even tasted my blood, and I'm still here."

I was pushing it now. I expected someone was going to lunge at me. It was a surprise when Bella was the one that reacted first.

She laughed. "You are pathetic. Your attempts at distraction are amateur hour." She barked commands at the other vampires, ending with, "Get them."

Once the vampires raced towards us, I pulled a green magic ball from my pocket. I hadn't had occasion to use this one. It was a nasty little surprise from the queen of nasty herself. I grinned and threw it at the largest group. They didn't have time to even look surprised. Poof. They were gone. Dana would enjoy a few playthings in her dungeon.

Unfortunately, I only had one, and it would only take three victims at a time. The others kept coming, although seeing their compatriots disappear in front of them made them stumble a bit. Mr. Mittens turned them to ash without even appearing to exert himself.

Then it was the three of us—numbers that were much more even.

Megan turned the corner at the perfect moment, and I said, "Now."

I threw everything I had at Amber, and Mr. Mittens leapt at her. The shield dropped just in time for Mr. Mittens' claws to bite into Amber's neck. One blow would have removed the head of almost everything living, and Amber was no exception. As her head spun away, Vic's horrified gaze followed it. Mr. Mittens came back to my side.

I smiled at Vic and Bella. "You have three choices. Turn and run, and I'll let Mr. Mittens play with you, stand there, and I'll send you to the Faerie dungeon your friends are sharing, or you can face me."

Megan had Excalibur and her shield out, and behind her were three wolves.

Bella transformed and flew away. Before she had gone too far, Mr. Mittens snagged the bat from the air. He kept a massive paw on her. She squeaked and wriggled until he unsheathed his claws, then she froze.

"Bella has chosen"—I made a show of looking at her—"Poorly." I gave Mr. Mittens a brief nod, and in an instant, the bat was a smudge of dust.

"Have you made a decision?" I asked Vic one more time. His gaze was fixed on the spot where Bella had been.

"I choose…" He moved vamp fast and came hurtling towards me.

Chapter Forty-Three

Mr. Mittens was faster. Before Vic could slam into my unprotected chest, Mr. Mittens jumped in and collided with the vamp. Vic went flying back. It gave me the seconds I needed to pull up my power. Thirteen braided elements exploded from my hands, and Vic vanished in a spray of ash.

I collapsed on my boulder.

Megan rushed over to me. "I was too late!"

I shook my head. "No, your timing was perfect. We needed that distraction. Thank you."

She put her weapons, once more magic balls, in her pocket and hugged me. "I thought that...when Vic was hurtling at you..." She shuddered. Although she hadn't finished her sentences, I understood what she was saying. She'd been in the path of danger often enough. I knew the fear she felt, personally.

"I'm exhausted," I said simply.

She sat next to me, the boulder barely large enough. "Yeah."

Mr. Mittens came and sat in front of us. He yawned. I guessed he was tired, too. He picked up a paw to clean it of vamp dust, noticed how dirty he was, and did something I would never expect. He waded into the waterfall pool, submerged himself, and let the water carry away however many hundreds of vampire's worth of dust that had worked its way into his fur.

He exited, his tawny coat showing the black rosettes in sharp outline, and shook.

"Dammit, Mr. Mittens! I was dry!" Megan yelled.

I sputtered, but I was so dirty and disgusting that the water was just an added inconvenience. I sighed.

Once he was done, he stood there before us as he shrunk back to Ragdoll form, perfectly clean and dry. *Hmpf, you should watch where you stand, then,* he said with his usual disdain.

I chuckled. I was too exhausted to give the true laugh the situation demanded.

Megan wiped her hands down her clothes. "Ugh!"

He jumped on the boulder and folded himself into my lap.

I patted him absently, scratching where he aimed himself at my hand.

"I'm so tired," I said again.

Megan grunted in agreement. I guessed she was tired too. The three wolves that came up with Megan, started to whine, Megan sat up sharply. "We have to go; something is wrong."

I slid off the boulder and brushed off my pants. "I can walk us. Everyone, gather round and touch me."

Megan, who had done this before, grabbed my arm. The three wolves leaned against my legs, and I walked us back to the house. Mr. Mittens walked himself.

We landed in my parking lot, and the wolves started to run for the trees in the back of the parking lot. I looked around. The vampires were dead. Merlin had landed with the red dragon and was standing next to him in the parking lot, talking to my grandfather and the gargoyles. I looked around for Gabe, but I couldn't see him anywhere. My heart nearly stopped, and my throat closed off. Where was he?

Megan was already four or five steps ahead of me, so I tore off at a run, following.

Mr. Mittens was in between us, his floof pressed back with his speed. The feeling of dread in my guts grew with each step.

My heart pounded with fear and sweat poured off my head and dribbled into my eyes. I ran for all I was worth, even managing to almost catch up with Megan, although she was in better shape than I.

We slid to a stop somewhere in my woods. Two bodies lay on the ground, surrounded by vamp ash. Gabe was leaning up against a tree, his forehead bloody, his skin ashen, and his eyes closed.

"No, no, no!" I ran up to him and checked his pulse. It was slow and uneven. I reached into my pocket. I still had three healing balls. I shoved my fingers in his mouth and opened his jaw. Then I shoved the ball to the back of his throat, none too gently, and forced it down.

I looked over at the other body. It was a wolf. I left Gabe, knowing he'd be fine. The healing ball would do its job.

I had to get another ball into the mouth of the wolf.

"It's Luke," Megan said.

I could hear the fear in her voice and see it in the tension of her posture. She knelt next to him, brushing his fur with her hands. I looked closer. He was soaked in blood.

"Help me get this healing ball into him," I said gently and moved down next to his head. I knelt beside Luke and pushed his muzzle up so I could open his mouth.

Megan sobbed, quietly.

With my hand on him, I felt his life ebb away. Luke took a shuddering breath and stilled. His body shifted back to human form.

I was too late. He was gone.

Megan threw herself over his body, the horrendous wounds too visible on his human skin. His family howled their grief. I sat frozen, the healing ball in my hand dropped to the ground, useless. It could heal the most terrific wounds, but it couldn't bring back the dead.

I stared at the body, at Megan, unable to move, unable to comprehend the brutality of our loss. This was Luke. He'd been there for me from the beginning. I pictured his warm smile, his comforting presence, his humor, his fierce love for Megan.

I stood and pulled Megan away from the body. She was inconsolable, sobbing so hard she gasped for air. I held her. The Whelans surrounded their fallen brother, mourning him as wolves do, their howls full of their aching love and loss.

I had all the magic in the world, and I couldn't get here in time. Time. My heart began to race.

I caught movement from the corner of my eye. Gabe was coming around. The magic healing ball had worked. He took in the scene, my face, Megan's uncontrollable weeping. Luke. He knelt next to Luke. And pressed his hand to Luke's head, stroking his blood-soaked hair.

"He saved me," Gabe said.

I realized I'd also been crying, but that simple statement ripped my guts out. Luke had sacrificed himself keeping Gabe safe. I owed him my everything.

I looked at my friends and took a step to the practice planet. I had to try. I aimed for when we were still at the waterfall waiting for Vic. That should be far enough away I wouldn't rebound by meeting myself. I stepped back into the clearing.

My breath caught. Gabe was alone and surrounded. He'd been out of fireballs for a while, but he had a bainca-pall spear in his hand. Unfortunately, he had to be close to the vamps to use his magic. He swung and stabbed the spear at his opponents. He'd ashed several. His face intent, he looked as though he fully intended to take every vamp with him. I zapped three that got to close, but something struck me from behind. I went down. Gabe hadn't noticed me, not that he could do anything about it. The vamp who had surprised me was biting me, the bastard.

I walked, and when I landed on the practice planet, the vamp stumbled, confused. I ashed it with a lightning bolt and walked back. Gabe was slowing, and the vamps were milliseconds from winning. That's when Luke sailed in. He was amazing to see—a silver blur as he whirled, dealing death to the vamps. He whined a few times, vamp claw marks scoring his sides.

I threw my magic in carefully, trying to eliminate enough vamps to save Luke. I kept it up, until my own presence became too close, forcing me back to the time I'd left. I'd failed. I looked at Luke's body, back in the right time, and sank to my knees.

Noah shifted back to his human form. He and Gabe picked up Luke's body gently, and we followed them back to the house, overwhelmed with our grief.

All talking and celebrating ended when we came within sight of the house. The baincapall, Fae, gargoyles, and Merlin stopped and watched us in respectful silence. We laid Luke on the back porch, and Noah covered him with a blanket from his truck.

Megan was in such a state, that Gabe grabbed a sedative from his first aid kit and gave it to her. Picking her up, he carried her into the house. Soon enough, she fell asleep in her own bed. I knew if I were her, I'd want to remain sedated until I couldn't think anymore—blissful oblivion was the first step to healing. Not that she wouldn't carry this for the rest of her life. I knew I would.

Chapter Forty-Four

It was touch and go with Megan for the first few months after Luke's death. Nothing interested her. Not her weapons, not dragon riding. Poor Goch tried to comfort her, tried to get her to go flying or interest her in anything. She ate, she answered phones and sat at the desk—once the guests returned—then she slept almost every other minute of the day we didn't keep her occupied.

As her best friend, even I couldn't engage her. I tried everything I could think of to bring back the exuberant love of life she'd always had. None of my attempts worked. I was desperate, and I tried everything from vacations, spa days, movies, everything I know she loved. I even took her to Faerie to see if the baincapall could bring her out of her sadness.

Of all the people who you wouldn't expect could pull her from her depression, it was Merlin that managed it.

He'd fulfilled the obligations that I'd somehow gotten him involved in. Then he decided he was going to be my teacher. I still needed to fulfill my promise to the griffins before I was free. We'd been working with my grandfather to expand the link to Faerie for the griffins. It was long and grueling work, but in doing it, I learned infinite more control and more about enchanting.

One day, while Merlin was at the inn, giving me a lesson on enchanting, he asked me about Megan.

"Brigid, do you trust me?" he asked.

"I do now," I answered and was surprised to see that I really did. He'd become another friend in the short time I'd known him.

"I'm worried about your friend." He watched her sitting at the reception desk, staring at nothing.

"I am, too."

"I believe I can help."

I looked at him with surprise, and at the same time, gratitude. I'd let him try anything if it would bring her back to herself.

He walked boldly up to her, and he said something to Megan that lit a fire in her belly. Neither of them would tell me what it was. Megan only said that she would tell me when she was ready, but she added that she hated him with the intensity of a thousand suns.

Merlin reminded me to trust him. What he'd done, wasn't his to share, but Megan's. And to remember that his long life had made him a good judge of character.

I couldn't argue with Merlin, because after that, Megan decided it was her destiny to prove something to him.

She started flying with Goch again. I don't know what they did or where they went. She often came back looking as though she'd been through a fight, although Excalibur's sheath made sure she wasn't wounded. For all I knew, they were walking the splinters or doing vigilante work.

After a year, she seemed to be almost back to her old

self. She was still prone to bouts of depression, but her humor, plucky attitude, and fascination with the supernatural world returned. I quit feeling like I needed to keep an eye on her, afraid she was one bad day from suicide.

I was grateful for her change, because with the threat from the witches and vampires eliminated, my business thrived. I had little time to do much else but run it, and I needed all the help I could get. I gained clients from all over Earth, and my clientele from Faerie grew as well. Mr. Mittens kept the woods free from dangerous critters, and I was able to send Sorcha and the baincapall back to Faerie with purses full of Fae gold soon after the last battle.

Without enemies to worry about and the inn running smoothly, we decided it was time to plan the wedding. However, we wanted Megan to be a part of it, so we waited until she was more stable. Every time she looked at my ring or saw Gabe kiss me, the depression seemed to grip her harder. Gabe knew that she was closer to me than a sister, and I needed her to be whole before I could enjoy my own happiness. So, the waiting was only painful because we felt her pain so keenly.

Almost a year from Luke's death, and a few months after whatever Merlin had said to her, we felt that she'd healed enough that we could finally go ahead with the wedding. I was surprised when Megan wanted to be involved with the planning, but she loved me enough to put aside her grief.

She wanted to decorate the house for the wedding and arrange everything, and since she'd never have the wedding she'd dreamed of with Luke, I didn't mind. I was having the wedding of my dreams, and I knew someday when she was ready and had met another man as wonderful as Luke, I'd return the favor.

Epilogue

The only thing Megan left for me to do was find "the dress." For my first wedding, we'd both been poor, just out of school, and I wore the best dress I had for our ceremony at city hall—which wasn't much. This time, I had wealth and much better taste than I had back then.

I wasn't interested in anything traditional, not after seeing the amazing clothing in Faerie, so Megan and I took a trip for a visit with the court designer. I gave the designer very loose ideas of what I wanted and let her work her magic.

I really don't know if she used magic past her own talent with a needle; she might have, but what she came up with was amazing. I wanted something to show off my grandmother's sapphires, and my engagement ring. The dress she created was perfect. It was silver with an ever so slight blue iridescence when I moved. It was like the color of supercooled ice. It made my hair glow like fire and my eyes pop. Coupled with the sapphires, I looked and felt like a queen. After my hair was done in an elaborate Fae arrangement with sapphire pins dotting it, I could have been mistaken for royalty.

The inn was closed except to wedding guests. And I was blessed to have all my friends and family present. My grandfather agreed to perform the ceremony. Mr. Mittens even agreed to walk me down the aisle. We used a mix of Earth and Fae wedding traditions.

The day of, I sat at my vanity, touching up my makeup, and getting ready to put on my dress. My hair had already been arranged artfully and looked somewhere between sculpted and windblown but still amazingly beautiful. The red seemed brighter, and my skin glowed.

I stared at myself. Sometime during the past two years, and probably since I'd reintegrated my magic and used it nearly constantly, I'd stopped looking entirely human. I had the glowing skin and hair of one of the high Fae.

When this had all begun, I couldn't imagine where it would take me. I'd never imagined that I'd reconnect with my childhood love, that I'd have a great-grandfather who was not only still alive, but young and hale. That I'd find new friends who I held to my heart as dear as any family. But I had that now. My heart swelled with love and happiness.

Megan entered the bathroom. "Are you ready for the dress?"

I stood and looked her in the eye. "I love you, Megan Findlay. You are the best friend anyone could ever have."

I blinked back tears; I didn't want to smear my makeup.

She smiled and hugged me, gently, so she didn't muss my hair. "I love you, too."

I nodded and stepped into my dress. Megan helped me arrange and fasten it, and I was ready.

She wore a flame red dress that matched Goch's scales.

The only theme of the wedding was bright colors. Megan had covered everything in sprays of flowers in a riot of color. The Fae adoration for color and iridescence was present in all the court clothing my Fae guests wore. Sorcha, with her dark hair and eyes, was stunning in shimmering gold. My grandfather, who was the tamest, still wore peacock blue, which set off his hair and eyes, so similar to mine. Even Dana had dressed in court finery, her dress cycling through shimmering shades of green and blue, which complemented her green skin and hair.

My earth friends were drab in comparison—the remaining Whelan brothers in black tuxedos, and Izzy and Madison in different shades of green. Anna, their mother was lovely in ivory.

Chef Jack looked good in a navy-blue suit, but Jim looked like someone was strangling him in his nicest jeans and a new western shirt which he'd added a bolo tie to. He wore his normal boots, only he'd given them a good clean and shine.

Goch attended, his scales sparkling. Brightfeather with her silver feathers neat and tidy, her half-grown chicks excitedly bouncing around, made my heart soar.

Mr. Mittens had been washed and brushed until he shone in the sun. His fur always was a little shimmery and glowed brightly. He wore a bowtie that matched my dress.

Once everyone was settled, Mr. Mittens and I walked down a path Megan had installed just for this. My grandfather waited at the end of the path as did Gabe. I'd expected Gabe to be wearing a tuxedo as well, but he was dressed in the Fae style with flowing robes and soft boots.

Gabe's hazel eyes were dark with his feelings. Looking at him standing there, waiting for me, struck me suddenly. Everything that had befallen me—from the abuse I had endured, the loss of my ability to have children, the crushing blow of having my husband toss me aside for a pregnant and younger model, the fight for my magic and life with the witches and the vampires, the sacrifice and struggle—was worth it. All for this moment.

I gazed back into his eyes as I said my vows. It was the most magical thing I'd ever done, and when he said his back, the love that poured form him was palpable.

I knew Gabe loved me with all his heart. I loved him back fiercely. In the short time since we'd reunited, we'd been through a lot, and I trusted him with my heart and knew he'd keep it safe. Instead of crying through my wedding, I couldn't stop smiling.

After the ceremony, we had a glorious party. Megan and the Whelan's did a great job hiding their grief, although it would always be there for them as well as for me. They had lost a husband, father, brother, and son. The most of all of us. I couldn't believe they were still fierce friends and part of the family I now claimed as my own.

I was showered with gifts both mundane and practical, as well as magical and amazing. Merlin made me a magic energy storage device of my own—no slave function involved. It was a simple ring, so I didn't have to worry about it chafing my neck. The dragons gave me an immense, uncut sapphire to use in my magic. The gargoyles gave me an original Leonardo da Vinci drawing, one that had never been seen. The griffins brought me a history of their people, beautifully illustrated and hand illuminated.

My grandfather gave me a Faerie castle near his own, so we could have a place to visit and if we wished, live in. I thought about it. We were content for now with our place on earth, the B&B and Gabe's practice, but we might grow tired of it. The promise of a new adventure would always be welcome.

Mr. Mittens told me he didn't have things to give, which I knew to be true, he was a cat after all. It made me feel horrible that he was sad that he didn't have a wedding gift to offer.

I pulled him aside. "You have given me the best gift possible. You have been my protector, my friend, and my truest companion. I can't imagine having anything more precious than that."

He gave me a head butt and purred loud and long. Seeing his eyes full of love was gift enough.

We partied hard into the night. And when the last guest had departed, I looked at Gabe, Megan, and Mr. Mittens and knew my life was complete.

More by Jilleen Dolbeare

vinci-books.com/shadow-winged

Soaring through Alaskan skies, Piper Tikaani thought she knew danger. Then the ancient gods returned, hunting her kind.

In a world where ancient gods return and shadow-winged shapeshifters are hunted, Piper Tikaani, an Inupiaq Raven Clan bush pilot, finds herself entangled in a deadly mystery. When a friend is found dead, she uncovers hidden treasures and terrifying truths about her clan and herself. Somehow, Piper must survive the ice age were-predators determined to see her dead.

Turn the page for a free preview…

Shadow Winged: Chapter One

The rugged cliffs of the Alaska Range darkened as the clouds pressed from above. I decreased my air speed and descended another hundred feet, hugging the right side of the steep mountain and giving myself room in case I had to turn around in the narrow pass and go back to Anchorage. We were close enough to the side of the mountain to observe a band of grizzlies under my right wing. Most of the animals cringed when we buzzed past, but a huge boar looked up, challenging us. My client barked out a quick laugh.

I'd already sunk four hundred feet on my way through the pass, and we flew along at an altitude of eight hundred. The lowering ceiling kept forcing us down as I raced an incoming front. I cleared the pass and zoomed out over open ground, trees, and tundra.

Suddenly, a black cloud materialized in front of me. I slowed further, trying to dip below. As I grew closer, I realized it was a cloud of dark birds. My heart sped up. I dipped my right wing to avoid them, but they moved almost as if they were *trying* to hit me.

I increased the dip further, and accidentally stalled the wing—losing lift. We dropped fast. My passenger gasped loudly. I grimaced; teeth clenched with concentration. After some quick maneuvering, I recovered from the stall, sweat running down my back.

A flash of black feathers and a loud whump were all I saw as the ravens bounced off the plane. "Shit!" I yelled as I dove further to avoid the rest. We were down to three hundred feet. The clouds were still pressing on us, and I worried about the damage the large birds might have caused the cloth covered Super Cub.

"We're going to have to land." I straightened out and looked for somewhere to put down. "I need to assess the damage."

He grunted affirmatively. Rough maneuvering like that can leave your passengers a bit green, so I hoped he was doing well and wouldn't spray my cockpit with vomit.

Luckily, we were over a river and even though it seemed to be running higher than usual, there had to be a gravel or sand bar somewhere big enough to land a good bush plane on. The Cub bounced and swayed in the strong wind, and the sky continued to threaten as I located a potential landing spot on a gravel bar.

A quick glance back showed my passenger's white knuckles clinging to the back of my seat. I buzzed the gravel bar twice, mentally checking the length, and circled back to land. I came in at an angle, fighting the crosswind, and straightened at the last second to avoid the possibility of the wind flipping us. I could smell the sharp, quick scent of fear. Mine and the stranger's. It filled the plane as the sudden deceleration pushed us into the seat belts.

The Super Cub is the workhorse of the bush. It's small, likes to fly, carries a good load, and can take-off and land in a very short distance—luckily. I dragged my oversized Bush-wheels through the water, slowing the plane, and bounced gently down the short, makeshift runway. I turned and maneuvered it for a quick take-off before I powered down.

"You doing okay back there?"

I got another affirmative grunt.

"You might as well stretch your legs; I know it gets a bit cramped back there."

I pulled off my headset and opened the door. The wind tore my long braids free and whipped them around my head. I cursed quietly and grabbed my red Tulugaq cap and jammed it down firmly, holding my hair in place.

"That was some pretty good flying." His voice was husky, deep, and rumbled from his chest.

I shrugged. I wasn't happy with my flying right now. "It's like they came out of nowhere." I scowled up at the darkened sky. "It's weird. I thought ravens were too smart to hit a plane," I spoke quietly, mostly to myself.

I didn't let on about it freaking me out. Ravens are a personal animal for me. Hitting them made me feel slightly nauseous and unbalanced.

I helped him remove the bags and gear that were pinning him down, and he stepped out.

A quick chill raised the hair on my neck and peppered me with gooseflesh. I looked around to see if anyone besides my passenger was around. No one. I brushed off the feeling. How dumb, by worrying about the ravens I'd spooked myself!

I frowned slightly at my passenger, trying to remember his name. He had a bemused smile on his face. He pushed his hat back a little. His auburn hair was peeking out, some pressed against his head with sweat. He pulled off his sunglasses and rubbed his face. When he looked up, his bright blue eyes immediately drew me in. Wow. He hadn't looked more than average at first glance, but those eyes were something. I looked away quickly.

He took a deep breath of the cool, clean air and looked around. "I can see how this country can get under your skin," he said. "Can I help you with anything?" he added after turning back to me.

"Thanks, uh, Vanice?" I stumbled through the name, hoping I'd got it right. I thought for a moment longer; no, that was right, Vanice Fletcher, but he had some kind of nickname. He flinched; I should have paid closer attention to dad when we were loading up.

"Call, me Fletch or Fletcher," he said. "Vanice was my grandfather."

"Okay, sorry. I'm Piper, by the way, like my airplane. It's a Piper Super Cub. Only I'm Piper Tikaani. I was a little distracted before. I don't remember if I told you my name." I was babbling. I shut my mouth, held out my hand, and we shook. "I'm good, with the plane, I mean. Why don't you have a look around while I check it over? Just keep an eye out for bears."

"Sure."

As he wandered away, I looked for damage. There didn't seem to be any marks, blood, or feathers on my propeller, which was good; I didn't think the ravens hit it, and I hadn't heard any change in the engine. I checked the leading edge of my wings. There was a small tear in the fabric on the right wing. I got out a roll of duct tape and fixed it. It wasn't pretty, but it would get me to Vanice's, ugh, Fletcher's cabin and back home. I didn't see anything else other than some blood down the side. I wiped it off. We were good.

I got in, pulled on my headset, tuned the radio to our air service's private channel, and pushed down the talk button on my throttle. "Tulugaq base, dad, pick me up?"

"Yeah, I got you, Pipe, okay."

"Hey, dad, we had a bird strike, Cub's fine. I had to put us down forty-two miles north- northeast of Clyde's. The front has pushed the ceiling and visibility down, and we're going to be hustling to the cabin. Would you please have mom or Baylee call and see if they can get me a later hair appointment tomorrow? I don't know if I'll make it back tonight, okay?"

"Sure thing, Piper, dad out."

I was delivering my passenger to an old family friend's cabin who had died this past fall. Fletcher had inherited it from Clyde and had never been there before. I turned off the radio and climbed back out.

I groaned inwardly. This was my third drop off flight of the day, and I was ready to be done. All I wanted was something warm in my belly and to stretch out on my comfortable bed.

The wind amped up even more. I looked up, concerned at what I saw. The clouds bore down, and the sky grew heavier and darker. I radioed Anchorage and got a weather report.

"Damn," I mumbled to myself. "Fletcher?" I called out tentatively, still not sure about his name.

"Yeah, I'm over here." He waved his hand at me from the brush over by the tree line about fifty yards back from the river.

His neutral clothing blended in well. He wore a tan shirt and faded blue jeans. He seemed to be five ten or eleven. I was average height for a woman, so he was probably only a few inches taller than me. He started back. Just then, I saw him jump to the side and whirl back to look at the tree line. I walked over to join him, concerned. I scanned the tree line to see what made him jump.

"Someone threw a rock at me." The sunglasses were back down over his eyes.

Raven gives me better eyesight than anyone I know, but there wasn't anything to see through the trees and the brush. I took in a deep breath to see if I could pick up a foreign scent.

Just then, a loud noise came from behind us and to the left, a *thwack* like wood being struck against wood. We both turned and faced that direction, spooked. I didn't have my weapon; it was in my backpack back in the Cub, but I reached behind me to the holster that I usually kept there when I was in the bush.

Thwack, thwack, thwack, again, this time rhythmically and quick. It was about five hundred feet in yet another direction; the wind had shifted, so I still couldn't pick up a scent. The hair on the back of my neck stood up. I was sure we were being watched.

"It's too loud for a woodpecker, or a ground squirrel," I mumbled.

He grunted an affirmative. We walked faster back to the plane. Fletcher's hand was behind his back, and I wondered if he had a weapon within reach like I should. I kept catching movement out of the corner of my eye, but when I turned to look, nothing was there. A large rock landed to the left of us. We picked up the pace.

"I think someone is screwing with us," Fletcher growled.

"Who?" I asked.

There wasn't anyone here for miles. No cabins. I hadn't seen any other aircraft from the air, although it was possible some hunters had this area staked out and were trying to scare us off, but I hadn't seen any signs when we flew over. Bears don't throw rocks, though.

I quickly got Fletcher resituated in the back seat, and all the gear packed back in. I climbed in and pulled on my headset, checked that Fletcher was wearing his, and flipped the intercom system on.

"The weather report stated that the ceiling is down to five hundred feet and visibility is below one mile, we're going to have to go fast or stay here for the night. It'll be rough. Are you ready?"

His answer was immediate. "Yes."

Just as I was about to shut the door, I thought I heard an unrecognizable, eerie howl. It sent a primal shiver down my spine, but I shrugged it and the feeling of being watched off as the wind and my overactive imagination. I pulled my door shut securely and fired up the engine. I blasted down the short gravel bar and the Cub lifted fast into the air, the wind screaming over the wings.

There are a few unwritten rules of the bush pilot. One is to never fly too low with a client. Alone, I had no qualms pushing myself or my ride, but it's safer to have extra air between you and the ground in case anything happens— like the raven incident.

I'd have to skim the bottom of the clouds to get us to the cabin, but I figured it was worth the risk to make it to shelter before the storm opened up and stranded us in the wilds with whatever had stalked us.

I fought the wind all the way to Fletcher's cabin. Luckily, I could see the landing strip before the low ceiling and the wind forced us out of the sky once again.

A landing strip in the bush is not a paved or even an oiled dirt road; it's equal to a cleared area where there may be a smoothed-out section, or it may just be mown grass, gravel, or a break in the trees. Clyde's strip was well used in the past, but it hadn't been tended to for over ten months. Granted, most of that was winter, and it was early enough that the grass that was growing wasn't very long. There was still snow hanging on in patches amongst the trees, but no brush had quite covered the strip yet. I circled it and scrutinized it thoroughly for branches or other debris before I put down.

Fletcher was quiet the whole way. Not because he was uninterested in talking, but to let me work through the turbulence. Now, we sat and listened to the pinging of the cooling engine. The trees blocked the wind somewhat, but an occasional gust would rock the small plane.

I radioed Tulugaq and let dad know we were here. The ceiling had dropped again, and it looked like the front that seemed to want to blow past had decided to drop a wallop of a storm after all. I'd be staying until morning. I sighed. Why did I bother making a hair appointment, anyway? I'd just make do, as usual, with hot rollers and charm for my date tomorrow night.

I huffed out a small laugh at myself, like charm was anything I had to offer.

I was shaky from fighting the stick the last forty or so minutes, and I was starving from the calorie draw. I pulled off my headset and opened the door to help Fletcher unload and get out. We secured the aircraft and started hauling his gear to the cabin.

The cabin was old, but Clyde had done some work to modernize it. It originally had one small window in the front by the door. He'd cut a window into each wall and added good, insulated glass, which slid open and had screens. The door was sturdy, handmade, solid wood.

Logs are naturally very insulating, but when Clyde had replaced the sod roof, he'd added more peak and insulated under the steel. He'd covered the inside of the roof with boards I'd hauled in with my plane. The floor was also wood, and since the cabin was older than Clyde's time, I'm sure that originally it had been dirt. He had a wooden framed bed in the far corner with a thick memory foam pad; I'd brought that to him. It was a lot more comfortable for aging bones than the old camp pads he'd used for years.

The other main corner had his stove. Clyde'd had steel flown in and built his own cook stove. Clyde liked to cook and can. He kept his kitchen area clean and neat, and the stove was a piece of functional art. You filled it with wood, and it doubled as a heater. He kept a small kerosene heater as well; I assume for when it got too warm using the stove. He had a small wooden table, two wooden chairs, and a wooden rocking chair next to a small bookcase, all hand made. There was electricity wired to the house, one outlet, an overhead light above the kitchen, and a lamp by the chair. He kept various things hanging on the walls, furs, a moose rack, some old photos—dad had taken most of those —and shelves with various things. It was a well lived-in home.

When we walked in, it smelled a bit musty from being shut up for such a long time. It was dusty and damp. Dad had locked everything up and taken care of any perishable foodstuffs by taking them out to burn, so it didn't smell of any rot; however, it was going to need a good scrubbing just the same.

I wrinkled my nose. "Maybe we should open the windows for a short time and air this place out."

"Good idea," Fletcher agreed.

I opened the windows. I knew we wouldn't be able to keep them open long, the temperature was dropping too fast, and the wind was still ramping up. I dug through my stuff for the matches and gathered wood to start a fire in the cookstove. Clyde had at least two years of split wood piled up along the house and shed, so it didn't take too much time or effort to build up a blaze. Clyde also had water piped to the house from the river, so I put a pot of water on to boil. Cocoa sounded good, something warm and sweet.

"I'm going to go have a look at that generator," Fletcher said after he finished stacking his gear neatly inside by the door. "I'll see if I can get it up and running."

I cleaned most of the surface dust away, washed off the table and chairs, and swept the floor while the water boiled. There wasn't much more cleaning that could be done without a day and a good scouring, but with the windows open and the bit of cleaning I'd done, the place smelled noticeably better. I have an extremely sensitive nose, so that was an instant relief. Plus, the cold wind dried out the collected moisture quickly. I was wearing my fleece-lined windbreaker, having left my heavier jacket in the plane. It was getting too cold to have the windows open, so I shut them.

Once the water was rolling in the kettle, I poured it into two mismatched, quickly cleaned mugs for the cocoa. The lights blinked on as I was stirring. Fletcher had gotten the generator running.

We'd brought up some lamp oil and candles, but we

knew Clyde had refilled his fuel storage before he'd died, so we didn't need to bring any other fuel with us. The extra light unveiled the cobwebs in the corners, and the dust that had collected on the inside of the logs. I tried not to let it bother me. It wasn't my place; I could live with the dirt.

With the windows closed, the place grew toasty quickly. My stomach rumbled, and I had the beginnings of that grouchy, lightheaded, "I need to eat soon" feeling. I don't let myself get too hungry; I have a lot less control over hiding my differences when I am. I pulled a military Meal Ready to Eat cheese tortellini entrée out of my backpack. Fletcher walked in with a blast of icy air as I sorted through my backpack for a candy bar.

"Wow, it's really picked up out there," Fletcher said.

I looked around; it had grown darker. I could hear the brush of tree limbs against the metal roof, and the rattle as debris blew clear.

"Do you think it might snow?"

I frowned. It wasn't out of the question even in June, but I didn't want to get trapped here if a major snowstorm came through. "I hope not, but I guess it's possible. The weather service predicted wind, followed by fog with a slight chance of precipitation." I handed him the other mug of cocoa. We sat at the small table. "I just boiled water, and I was thinking of opening an MRE. Are you hungry?" I asked politely, although I planned to eat whether I had company or not.

"Starved. Let me dig something out of my stash," he replied.

I heated my MRE as he mixed up some of his freeze-dried food.

"Did Clyde ever mention being afraid of something out

here?" he asked as we started tearing into the food like refugees.

"No, why?" I replied, curiously.

"Well, I've noticed a couple of odd things. First, look at the doors into this place." I glanced at the rear door that led to the woodpiles and outhouse, and then the door we had come in. "What about them?" They didn't look any different from the last time I was here.

"They're absolutely solid." He opened the door so I could see the edge. "They have a steel core. Look, why does he have these reinforced bars?"

He lifted the wooden bar and slid it into its slots after he shut the door. Clyde's doors had those old-fashioned steel brackets bolted into them and the cabin, with thick boards that slid into them. I just assumed he liked that look, and it was cheaper to make them than to buy some deadbolt set.

"Why did he need floodlights?"

I thought about it for a while. Even having something that needs a light bulb, let alone a generator and electricity in the bush, is beyond extravagant. Everything that can't be brought by river had to be flown in and was extremely expensive.

Fletcher continued, "The windows are also too small to allow anyone to crawl through them. They should be bigger to let in light."

"I don't know, maybe he liked the way it looked?" I said uncertainly.

"There isn't another cabin or person for miles. He built this place like a fortress. Who's going to break in?"

"I guess I just assumed all gold miners are a little paranoid."

"The shed is the same way. It's also built from logs. He has enough steel roofing out there he could have much more easily built a metal covered shed. Yet, it has the same handmade steel core doors, and wooden braces, same with the outhouse. Also, both have food and water stashes."

I frowned; how had I failed to notice those things during the many trips I'd made here? Especially since I'd spent my growing-up years exploring every inch of the property in my various forms.

"I just never thought about it. That is odd. I'll ask dad when I get back to town if Clyde had ever said anything to him. They were friends. He hasn't ever said a thing to me, though."

I thought a little longer; my rational self overruling the nagging, instinctual alarm in the back of my head, "There is a rational explanation for everything if you think about it. In the winter, it is possible to get lost in a whiteout from here to the shed or the outhouse; there probably should be an emergency stash of food and water if you get caught in one.

Also, Clyde was a craftsman. He liked to make things; the doors could simply have been something aesthetic and functional to him. Same as the logs, they all match, and you have to admit the place looks good because it's not all mismatched and rusty.

"He also liked to work with metal." I gestured around the room at the various handmade metal objects, like the stove. "The windows are small to conserve heat and the bars, well maybe they were the easiest way to secure the doors, short of going into town and buying a lockset. It also gets dark in the winter, maybe he had the floodlights just so he could see from here to the shed."

There, that made me feel better. Everything could be rationally explained, even though it was totally impractical and expensive to haul such things out to the bush.

Fletcher frowned. "Yeah, you're probably right. I guess the way he died is making me suspicious of everything."

"No worries. I will ask, though. I'm sure there isn't anything really mysterious, but you never know." I paused for a moment, not sure if I should continue. The primitive urges to hide and flee, flirting in the back of my head, were making me uncomfortable and antsy. So, I shared them. Logically.

"On the other hand, this area, around the lake, has a history of strange happenings, unexplained lights, glimpses of unknown animals, disappearances, UFOs. Lake Iliamna even has a monster like Loch Ness!" I said lightly, jokingly, anything to lighten the mood. Clyde's place had never felt spooky to me like some places could, but these observations of Fletcher's were turning the tide on that. It was time to change the subject.

"You know, if you want to solve a mystery, here's a good one. Clyde always paid us in small glass bottles of flour gold." I paused for dramatic effect. "He didn't always know when we were coming, so I know he kept a stash somewhere that was readily available. Also, he mined all the time. So, where's the gold?"

"You think he found enough to bother hiding?" Fletcher asked.

"Yes, so does dad. We spent a lot of time trying to guess where Clyde had his gold stashed. It wasn't serious like we would look for it; it was just fun to guess. These old gold miners are notoriously paranoid and overly protective of their stash. Not that I blame them with the price of gold like it is."

"The attorney mentioned Clyde had paid him with gold. He'd left enough with the attorney for his burial, and the taxes on this place, so I didn't have to come up with anything when I took it over," Fletcher said.

"I guess it is possible he spent whatever he found to survive, but I bet he has something stashed around here, hidden. It might be fun to look." I shrugged.

"It will give me something to do after I inventory everything and decide what I need." Fletcher was quiet for a while, thoughtful, then he looked around the cabin. "I feel sort of strange going through this man's things, living in his home, talking about him, and I don't even know what he looked like, but here I am a stranger, dissecting his life, living in his personal space."

I threw up a hand. "Hold that thought!" I grabbed my backpack and dug around. I'd slipped in a couple of photos of Clyde, thinking it would be nice to show them to the new owner, who I thought would be a relative of some sort, but then in the midst of all that had gone on today, I'd forgotten. I handed them to him.

"This is a picture of Clyde and dad the summer before last. They were fishing on Ship Creek for kings." I lifted an eyebrow in question. I didn't know if he knew what king salmon were, but he nodded. I let him examine it. "This one is Clyde, here, in front of my plane." I watched Fletcher study the photos for a minute, and I tried to look at Clyde with fresh eyes. He had always appeared to be a man haunted to me. His mouth was smiling in the photos, but his eyes were always sad, in pain. He never spoke of what had driven him into the bush, but it must have been devastating to fill his eyes with such despair.

"I have dad's police statement, about Clyde's death. I'm not sure if you want to read it, it's a little disturbing, and since then, my dad won't talk about it. Reading it is better than me trying to tell you everything that happened, even though I know you know the basics. Dad was quite thorough in describing exactly what happened. I thought it may be something you'd be interested in." I was nervous about showing the report to him. It felt personal, because dad explained his thoughts and feelings as well as the details of finding his dead friend. Still, I figured it was more Fletcher's business than mine at this point.

He took the paper gently from my fingers, glanced at me a moment, and bent his head to read. His face remained stoic throughout—even though I knew the content was disturbing.

"Your dad is a descriptive writer."

"Yeah, he doesn't talk much, but he gets a little wordy when he writes."

"Thanks, Piper. I appreciate you sharing this with me." He handed it back. I folded it and stuffed it back into my pack. "Did the police ever discover any reason why he was on the roof?"

"Just guesses, but the fact he had pulled up the ladder throws all their guesses off." I shrugged, tired of guessing and of wondering what had happened.

I hurriedly changed the subject. "You said you were a stranger. I thought you were Clyde's relative?"

He looked at me for a moment. "No. Clyde left everything to my grandmother. I don't know how they were involved. I'm the only one of my family left, so I inherited everything by default."

I didn't know what to say, so I nodded. "Any particular place you want me to sleep?" I asked, although my heart was set on the foam bed.

He gave me a sexy crooked smile, mischief glinting in his eyes, and I gathered up a short retort, when he said, "You have your pick of any spot," he paused. "On the floor." He laughed as I turned pink, anticipating some chauvinist remark.

Realizing what he said, I opened my mouth to tell him what I thought.

He chuckled. "You can take the bed, but I'd like to know what you thought I was going to say."

"I bet you would," I mumbled as I spread my sleeping bag out over the memory foam.

The morning found me waking up disoriented, too hot, and trapped. I lay still and tried not to panic as I attempted to orient myself. Slowly, it came back to me as I focused on the log wall. I was at Clyde's, no… Fletcher's cabin, in his bed, with his arm around me. I relaxed.

"What!" I thrashed. "Get off me!" I wiggled my bag to the bottom of the bed and stood up. "What do you think you're doing?"

"Well, I was sleeping, finally," He stated groggily.

"I thought you slept on the floor," I whined.

"I tried to," He yawned. "But between your snoring, and the stench down there, I wasn't having much success." He rubbed his face. "Then you turned over and faced the wall, and left that invitingly empty stretch of bed, so…here I am."

"I didn't think you'd try something like that."

"Like what? You were in your sleeping bag, and I was in mine. It's difficult to steal someone's virtue from inside a mummy bag."

I'd lost the argument. It was his bed, after all, and I was as alone in my sleeping bag as he was in his. It didn't keep me from glaring at him as I redressed in my bag from the clothes I'd shoved down at the bottom the night before. Sure, they get a few wrinkles like that, but they're toasty warm when you put them back on. After nearly dislocating my shoulders, I was redressed and free of the bag. I yanked on my shoes and my jacket.

"I'm going out to check on the Cub and the weather," I said as I pulled open the door. It was completely still outside. There was a light fog, but it was enough to make the silence eerie. I'd grown up here more or less. Never did I have as intense a feeling of being watched as I did now. The eerie silence felt sinister.

My radio call ensured that Anchorage was clear, so once the fog burnt off here, I was free to go. I took my time going back to the cabin, embarrassed at how I'd acted. I was mad at being spooked by the fog, and sad to abandon a place that felt like home to a stranger. So, I took my time looking over my plane, did my preflight, and checked on my repair job, all before heading back in.

"I'm sorry about the way I acted," I said as I walked in.

Fletcher was sitting on his bed, dressed, rubbing his hands over his face and hair to wake up. "Don't worry about it," he replied.

"I can leave as soon as this fog burns off. Why don't I load our numbers into your sat phone while we wait, so you can get a hold of us as you need?"

"Good idea. Harder to lose that way," he replied.

I loaded the numbers to Tulugaq, my satellite phone, and my personal cell into his sat phone so he could reach our flight service anytime. I stuffed my sleeping bag into its compression sack and picked up my small mess. "Do you want me to help you check out the meat cache before I go? I could hold the ladder." I was still trying to make up for biting his head off for no reason.

"Sure, at least I'll have an idea what I'm up against," he said with a smile.

I peered up at the meat cache, a good ten feet in the air above my head. The wind had stirred and picked up, slowly clearing the fog. It was blowing away from me, so luckily, I couldn't smell it, but I could imagine that it wouldn't be pleasant. Fletcher leaned the ladder he had brought over from where it lay against the house onto the small ledge that ran in front of the cache. I held it steady as he climbed up and opened the door to glance inside.

"It's empty," he yelled down at me.

"What? That can't be! I know it was full before Clyde died. Was the door secured?"

"Yes, it has the same mechanism as the house, just on the outside," he started down. "Go have a look."

Curious, I started up the ladder. There was no way that meat cache should be empty, unless Clyde had emptied it shortly before he died. It should be full of meat. I looked inside. I believed Fletcher, but I was still surprised it was perfectly empty. Only the long-gone whisper of old blood-stains and the slight smell of old blood remained. I climbed down.

"Well, at least you won't have to clean it out," I said as I shook my head. "That's just bizarre."

"He could have just cleaned it out before he died, planning for new meat," Fletcher said.

"I guess, but I swear dad said he helped Clyde put some fresh moose up there only a week before he died," I replied, but I could be off by a few weeks. It was hard to remember for sure.

"Maybe it went bad, and he disposed of it."

"Yeah, I'm sure it's no big deal. At least you don't have to deal with the stench."

He looked thoughtful and glanced back up at the cache, measuring its height with his eyes. "I am curious about one thing, though. Last night, on the floor, I got a distinctly rotten odor—somewhere between dead meat, burnt onions, and skunk—coming in on the wind from under the door. It lasted for some time, so I climbed up into the bed. Last night, I told myself it came from the meat cache. The question is, what was it?"

Shadow Winged: Chapter Two

I looked at my phone and groaned. "Five o'clock already!" I mumbled as I juggled everything over to one hand so I could unlock my door.

Raleigh was picking me up in one hour, and I hadn't had a shower in two days. Then there was my hair. I threw my wallet and packages onto the couch and started stripping on my way to the shower. At least my new dress was made from that knit, shiny stuff that never seemed to wrinkle. He was taking me to a restaurant and then the theater, and I didn't even own a dress, thus the shopping splurge.

I left it in the bag as I scrambled to get in the shower as fast as I could. It took forever for my hair to dry. Once unbraided, it fell past the middle of my back, thick and wavy. I hated to blow it dry since that dried it out so much, but I didn't have a choice. I scrubbed and shaved as fast as I could and dressed hurriedly so I could do something with my hair and face. Luckily my complexion was good, clear, and slightly tanned from working outside. I could do with the briefest of eye shadow, mascara, and lipstick. I dried my hair while the rollers heated up and brushed my teeth. I checked the time on my phone, down to twenty-five minutes. After I rolled my hair up and left it to cook, I went to put on my shoes. That's when I realized I had forgotten to buy any.

I had planned on buying a pair of maroon short-heeled Mary Jane's I had admired in the online circular I'd perused over the weekend, or if that failed some black ballet flats, since I rarely wore heels.

"Dammit, dammit, dammit," I mumbled as I kicked my discarded clothes over to join the rest of the dirty laundry pile and crawled into my closet looking for something I could walk in. I came up for air with a pair of strappy red sandals with four-inch heels I'd bought once in a delusional state—and the encouragement of a friend—and never worn. *Great, after walking from the parking lot to the restaurant, and then the block to the theater, I'd have to be hauled home in an ambulance. What stupid things women do for beauty!* I thought as I frowned at the shoes in my hand.

After I removed the rollers and finished my hair, I walked into the dining room to look myself over in the full-length wall of mirrors. My house was built in the seventies; it wasn't my decorating choice. Although my hair didn't have the movie star waves I was going for, it looked fine, dark curls brushing down my back and framing my oval-shaped face. My new black, wraparound dress accentuated my small waist and softened up my curves. It had three quarter length sleeves and fell just below my knees. I had been putting fake tanner on my legs for a week, so they had a nice glow, and I didn't have to deal with hose. I wore my diamond tennis bracelet—a gift from my parents—and a simple long rectangular moonstone pendant hung from a silver chain to rest between my breasts. I actually looked feminine and maybe a little elegant. The red stripper heels were a bit much, but they made my legs look good, anyway. I was finally ready, and I had three minutes to spare!

I flopped down in my oversized leather chair with a sigh. It felt good to be home for a minute. I knew if I had to wait too long, I would talk myself out of going. I looked at the clock on my phone. I didn't really know much about Raleigh. I'd met him coming and going at the airport. He was also a bush pilot, but he worked for one of the top companies. He usually worked out of Talkeetna, but since he had family in town, I ran into him occasionally. He always went out of his way to be nice to me, which isn't always the case being a woman in a man's world, and he treated me like an equal. That was his major selling point.

His neatly trimmed hair was dark blond with that natural sun-bleached look that outdoorsy people tend to have. He wasn't much taller than me, which was another reason I hated the red heels. His brown eyes, nothing like Fletcher's bright blue, were nice, warm. He seemed to be well put together, as far as I could tell. Most of the bush pilots I knew weren't dressing to make a fashion statement at work, considering our business requirements.

I leaned my head back in my comfy chair, careful not to muss my hair. He was a bit thin lipped for me, I mused as I imagined the rakish, crooked smile and the sexy, upturned corners of Fletcher's mouth.

I shot up in the chair. "What am I doing?" I said aloud. Here I was thinking about one man and going out with another! Again, I checked my phone for the time; it was two minutes 'til. My palms started sweating.

"What am I doing?" I mumbled to myself, again. I don't go out much. Mostly because I don't get asked out.

I'm not really a people person. I don't really trust anyone because of my little differences.

I can hide it. I don't have to shift; the moon doesn't affect me. I just have some odd quirks that are easier to hide if I concentrate, like that little bit of eye shine humans don't have in the dark and the extra senses. Sometimes I'm a little too quick or a little too strong for a human woman. But, like I said, if I'm paying attention, I can hide it. It's just that a real relationship would be difficult because I'd always be hiding the true me. Which is why I have no real relationships. Not that I've really had anyone knocking down my door. Still, I hope that someone might come along with whom I could share my secret.

I sighed. "Do I really want to do this?" I said aloud, seriously contemplating calling Raleigh and bailing. Fortunately, or unfortunately, I'm not sure which, the doorbell rang. I teetered over, grabbing my jacket as I went, and with a painted-on smile, opened the door.

———

Warm sunlight directly in my face woke me up the next morning. The sheets were tangled around me, and my hair was a noose around my neck. I was so tired last night that I hadn't bothered to braid it out of the way. I had to go into work at one, so this was my time to do what cleaning I felt like and wash my clothes. I contemplated going back to sleep as I lay there looking at the ceiling, but since I was out of underwear, I had to get up. The summer, even the beginning of the summer, was busy for bush pilots. I had to get up and at 'em regardless of the fact I didn't do mornings.

Sometimes I wished I had a useful power like telekinesis,

so I could do everything from bed. Unfortunately, being able to change shape didn't do much in the way of help except eliminate the opposable thumb. Since I needed that thumb to pour in laundry detergent and turn on the washing machine, it was no help at all.

Before work, I pulled out my last load and got dressed in my "uniform," as dad calls it, which amounted to broken-in jeans, a t-shirt with a blue, checkered, flannel shirt over it, and whatever weight of jacket the weather demanded. I braided my hair, put on a battered Tulugaq cap, and headed over nearly forty-five minutes early—so not like me. I wanted to talk to dad about the odd things that Fletcher had noticed and see if Clyde had confided any fears to him. I had to do a babysitting job on a new pilot today so I wouldn't really get a chance later.

Dad was on the phone, flipping through his calendar when I got there. Even though we're small, we've developed a good reputation with a couple of local hunting guides and outfitters, so we were nearly completely booked for the season. It looked like dad was going to fill up the few remaining slots.

"How was your date, Pipe?" Dad asked after he hung up. This was an object of either amusement or torture for him, I wasn't sure which. It made both of us uncomfortable to talk about my dating.

"Fine, dad." I shrugged, as embarrassed as he was.

"Are you going to go out with him again?" he asked with a straight, but pained face, fulfilling his fatherly duties as outlined by my mom. I was definitely not, but I really didn't want to talk about it with anyone. Especially since it was an unmitigated disaster.

"I don't know, Dad, probably not. I promise I'll call Mom, so you don't have to know," I said vaguely.

"Good." He looked relieved. He glanced at his watch and back up at me.

"I wanted to ask you something," I said.

"I wondered why you were early." He smirked.

I winced. I did have a pattern. "Come on, I'm not that bad."

"Yes, actually, you are."

It was an ongoing family joke that I was late for everything. It wasn't exactly true. Things just ended up getting in the way of my attention—often.

"Fletcher, you know, the guy I took out to Clyde's place." I clarified for Dad; he wasn't great with names. "He noticed some odd things out there, and I said I'd ask you if Clyde had mentioned anything weird happening at his place."

"You mean other than him dead on the roof?"

"Yes Dad, other than that." I rolled my eyes.

"Why?"

"Well, for starters, the doors have a steel core, and he built everything unusually sturdy. The flood lights, oh, and the fact that the meat cache was completely empty."

This time he looked up at me. "What do you mean empty?"

"Just what I said. I held the ladder while Fletcher climbed up to check out the mess, and it was empty, not a scrap of meat in it."

"That is odd." He frowned to himself, thinking.

"Did Clyde ever say anything to you about anything weird happening, or being afraid?"

"No, sweetie, he didn't. You know Clyde, he was always high-strung, maybe even leaning to paranoid, but he never said anything out of the ordinary for him." He thought for a minute. "You know everything can be

263

explained pretty easily, especially when you add in Clyde's gold paranoia."

"Yeah, I know, but Fletcher had me a little spooked when he started pointing things out. You're right, it's probably nothing." I could think that, but at the same time, Clyde's weird death pointed to something not quite right. It was just hard to know, considering there could be a logical explanation for even the way he died. I pushed it to the back of my mind for a while.

"So, is the 206 ready?" Dad asked. We were trying out a new pilot today. He was a low hour pilot with a fresh commercial license.

We had one mail contract, and since it was approaching hunting season, we usually took on an extra pilot. Since our last guy had graduated on to his next big job, we picked up a low hour pilot to give him the experience he needed. It was cheaper for us, and a pilot could be paid to earn his hours. I was the lucky sitter today, so I got to fly with him to make sure he was competent, comfortable with the plane, and familiar with the route before we turned him loose.

"I fueled it up, but I'll let him do the rest, and see what he's got," I replied.

I sat in my favorite folding chair in the office as I waited for the new pilot and scrolled through my phone. I had a couple of voicemails, so I hit the call button to listen to them. The first one was from my mom, of course, asking about my date. I rolled my eyes; I'd have to call her when I got back. I erased that message and listened to the second.

It was my best friend, Branwyn. She probably wanted to hear about my date, but knowing her natural intuitive self, I bet it was more. I skipped it for later.

The last message was from Fletcher. "Piper, this is Fletcher." I sat up straighter, my interest piqued. It was just him calling in with his list, and I mentally kicked myself for reacting to his voice. I still had time, so I picked up my logbook to update my entries.

A logbook is a valuable tool for a pilot. There is the official FAA logbook that keeps track of aircraft engine hours and maintenance. Most pilots keep another one to track their flight hours for licensure. In it, pilots make record of essential details from each flight: takeoffs, landings, distances, passengers, etc. I checked my book and made sure I logged my last flight. I like to add notes about my days as well, and it's faster than a diary although not as detailed. I was finishing up when the new pilot finally walked in.

"Hi, I'm Steve." He extended his hand to Dad. Dad shook it.

"This is Piper, she's going to go up with you, show you the ropes." Dad gestured over at me, and Steve turned to look.

Luckily for him, he had a good game face. Most men—however modern they think they are—look disappointed at getting a flying lesson from a woman. At least, that has been my experience.

"Hey, Steve!" I stood and shook his hand. "Welcome. Do you have your charts?"

He nodded.

"I'm sure you're familiar with the route. I'll just show you some landmarks—check out some tricky wind areas. This is just routine; you should be comfortable by the time we get back." I could smell his nervous sweat, so I added, "It'll be fun!" I laughed, trying to put him at ease, although flying around in an aircraft I was not piloting was the last thing I wanted to do.

Dad threw me a strained look. He knew I was trying too hard, but as long as Steve didn't know, I was good.

"Let's go!" I pushed open the door into the sunshine, trying to think my happy thoughts while repeating the mantra, *Just another new guy, it will be over soon.*

The flight seemed to last forever, but once I got back, I reported to dad about the new pilot, got him squared away, and updated my logbook.

After work, I headed the fifteen miles to my parent's house to pick up my sister and head to the gym. I honked outside the house, trying to avoid a confrontation with my mom about my date. Luckily, my sister was on the same wavelength, because she came barreling out the front door, carrying her gym bag, her ponytails bobbing behind her. My sister is the fair Irish child my mother always wanted. We looked like we came from different planets.

My father's Inupiaq. I'm light-skinned for a part-native, but still a lot browner than my super fair, Irish born mother. Baylee looked like she fell off the potato wagon. The native genes she got from my dad had completely passed her by in looks and in the Raven's gift. She was strawberry blonde, with peaches and cream skin, and the personality and build of a cheerleader. The only things we shared were green eyes and naturally wavy hair. Her eyes were light-colored, like clear glass, and mine were dark green and stormy.

She tossed her bag in on the bench seat and bounced in. "You better hurry, before Mom gets to the door and waves you down."

I didn't waste any time pulling away from the curb.

Grab your copy...
vinci-books.com/shadow-winged

About the Author

Jilleen Dolbeare writes urban fantasy and paranormal women's fiction. She loves stories with strong women, adventure, and humor, with a side helping of myth and folklore.

While living in the Arctic, she learned to keep her stakes sharp for the 67 days of night. She talks to the ravens that follow her when she takes long walks with her cats in their stroller, and she's learned how to keep the wolves at bay.

Jilleen lives with her husband and two hungry cats in Alaska where she also discovered her love and admiration of the Alaska Native peoples and their folklore.